To Aleks, you were the first man to make me feel seen. You have given me the love I deserve. Thank you for everything you do for me.

My editor, who turned this book from trash to treasure

For all the queer men who felt discarded by society. You are not trash.

Remember it is Garbage Can!
Not Garbage Cannot!

Also by the Author

The Monarch Children Saga
Dad Magic – Book one
Scarlet Rex – Book Two – Coming Soon

Monsters & MENaces
Can't Refuse Him – Book One
Accounting On Him – Book Two –
Coming Soon

CAN'T REFUSE HIM

A PARANORMAL SECOND CHANCE
MM ROM COM

B.J. TWIGG

Kindle ISBN: 978-0-9756226-1-2

Paperback ISBN: 978-0-9756226-3-6

Can't Refuse Him is a work of fiction. Names, characters, places, and incidents are completely fictional. Any resemblances to actual persons, living or dead, ghostly or ghoulish, events or locals is entirely coincidental.

E-Book Cover by Benjamin Twigg

Paperback Cover – LISartworks

First edition 2025

Content and Trigger Warnings

Whilst I have endeavoured to make the book not triggering, I recognise this book explores topics that may be sensitive or triggering to some people. Do take care when reading.

Topics include:

Murder
Violence – Physical/Sexual
Toxic Relationships
Trauma
Grief
Facing one's Death
Sexual Coercion
Body Horror
Use of F-Slur
Food/Trash Fucking (in description only)

"I went into *Can't Refuse Him* expecting a filthy (in more than one way) lighthearted romantic romp but what I got was a surprisingly heartfelt, heartbreakingly sweet story about two cursed souls who found their peace in one another. *Can't Refuse Him* is funny, gross, charming and an unexpectedly touching. Have some tissues handy (for more than one reason) when you read it." – *Poppy Fitzgerald, Author of Astray, Exile & Duress from the Birch Falls Series.*

"With an irreverent sense of humor reminiscent of Terry Pratchett, B.J. Twigg nonetheless writes poignant and heartfelt romance. He calls attention to the injustices of life, while reminding readers that the small shared moments are to be cherished. *Can't Refuse Him* is the trash-themed romance you never knew you needed." – *Regina Sage, Shark Romance Author of Ocean's Embrace, Sand's Caress, Ink's Grace & Ocean's Kiss.*

"*Can't Refuse Him* is beautiful, raw, inspiring, heartfelt, and endearing. These are words I never thought I would use about a trash monster romance, but when the author gives a garbage can such emotional depth its necessary. What an absolute pleasure to read and a reminder its garbage can, not garbage cannot!" – *The Labrarian, Chloe McCarthy, Award Winning Creator, Indie Supporter and Aspiring Author.*

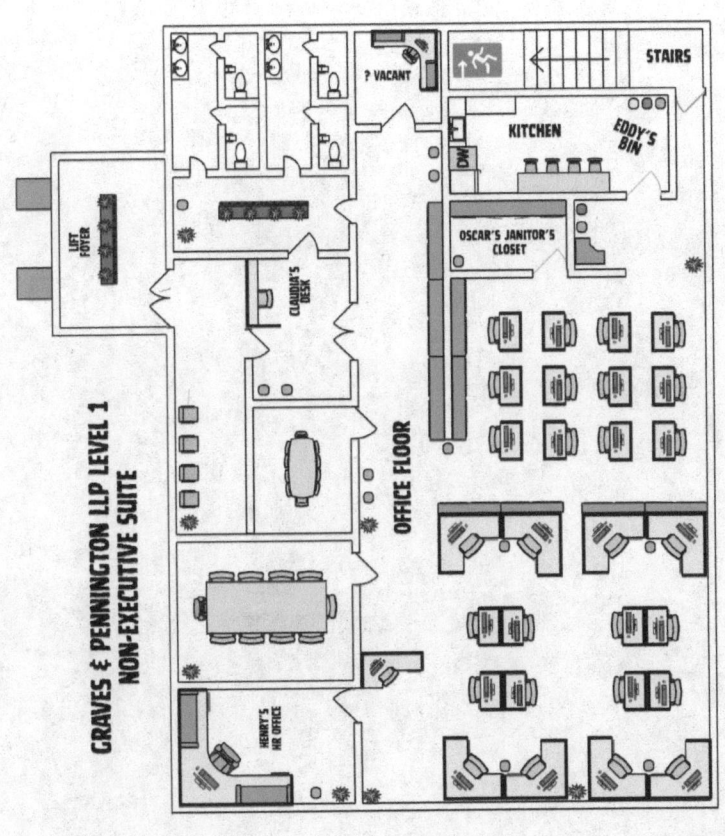

GRAVES & PENNINGTON LLP LEVEL 1
NON-EXECUTIVE SUITE

LIFT FOYER

? VACANT

STAIRS

KITCHEN

EDDY'S BIN

DW

OSCAR'S JANITOR'S CLOSET

CLAUDIA'S DESK

OFFICE FLOOR

HENRY'S HR OFFICE

Contents

OSCAR
"THE JANITOR"

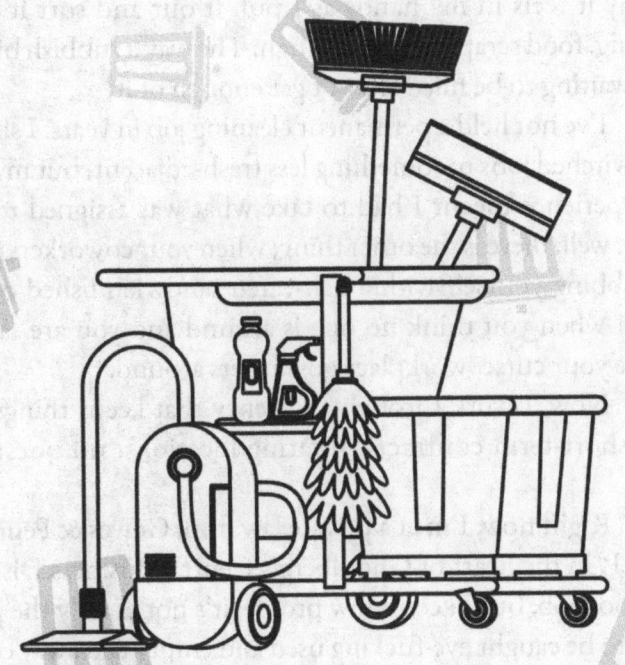

Chapter 1— The Spirit Within

S ome people hate their jobs; my job turns me on. Which, for a janitor, is just about the most humiliating thing imaginable.

I wasn't always like this—five years ago, a malicious ex laid a curse on me, and now I'm breathless over the aroma of day-old coffee grounds, ache at the sight of a perfectly crumpled and stained takeaway bag, and I get hot under the collar every time I take out the trash.

What used to repulse me now drives me wild—the smell, the way it feels in my hands as I pull it out and sort it from recycling, food scraps or refuse—ugh. The way a rubbish bin *sits there,* waiting to be filled–I can't get enough of it.

I've not held a permanent cleaning job in years. I should have switched jobs to something less trash-adjacent, but my limited experience meant I had to take what was assigned to me. Then... well, there is the other thing; when your coworkers catch you rubbing yourself with a half-eaten sandwich fished out of the bin when you think no one is around and you are safe to indulge your curse, workplace gossip gets around.

Now, I work through an agency that keeps things discreet–short-term contracts, rotating locations, no questions asked.

Right now, I'm at a private law firm, Graves & Pennington LLP, in the heart of Ghoulberg's Central Business District. It's a good job, but I keep a low profile; it's not exactly the place I want to be caught eye-fucking used and empty takeaway coffee cups. Don't get me wrong, I'm not an exhibitionist; it's just that

I can't control myself when I let my feelings go too far and the curse takes over. I keep my head down and do my job.

The law firm is eerily quiet today, more so than normal. Some people mill about, but they aren't chatty. It's the kind of place that smells like fresh money and expensive letterhead stationery. My footsteps echo against the polished floorboards as I wheel my squeaky cart of cleaning and maintenance supplies down the empty hallway. The sooner I finish what I came here to do today, the sooner I can go home and pretend my life isn't a complete joke.

Well, at least it's more entertaining now, with the revelation of the supernatural world being made public a few years ago. Zombies, vampiric himbos, marsupial shifters, demonic bakers and various other supernatural hauntings of the night have cropped up, and the last thing I want to face is any of those today. It's already hard enough controlling these urges.

I make it to the office kitchen where, aside from regular cleaning duties, I was given a job to inspect the faulty fluorescent lights. Hanging a 'maintenance' sign on the door, I shut it behind me. I flick the switch, and, after a hopeful flicker, it cuts out. No further response or light. The only thing illuminating the room is the green glow from a nearby exit sign–there are no windows. I try to ignore the eerie feeling I get as my eyes adjust to the dark. The dust of the day reflects off my glasses lens. I make a mental note to clean them on my shirt later.

As my eyes focus, I hate that the first thing I notice is a row of full, almost overflowing rubbish bins, seemingly waiting for me like a damn temptation lineup. General waste, recycling, organic waste–each one brims with discarded leftovers from people who actually have careers. My throat goes dry as I reach for the closest bin, swallowing hard against the awful *thrill* creeping up my spine.

Don't react. Just do the job.

I glimpse my name tag's reflection on the bin lid–Oscar. *Come on, Oscar, you've got this.*

I grab the plastic liner and–oh, *fuck.*

It's warm, and I want to shove my hand inside. It makes my stomach flip. I lose all control of my body. My glasses slip down my nose. I feel a tightening under the waistband of my briefs. The collar of my janitor's uniform feels like it is strangling me. My fingers instinctively clench around the bag, but I can't let the moment progress.

I take a steadying breath and grip the edge like it's a lifeline. I picture safe thoughts: puppies, clean countertops, new books. Ones that will bring down my desire, and my anxiety of having to work with trash and be around people who might see me getting turned on by it. For a second, it works, and the feeling subsides. But then, I feel the bag almost grip me back.

I yank my hands away from it so fast I nearly tumble backwards.

The fluorescent tubes above me suddenly flicker, and an ominous gust of air rattles some dishes drying nearby on the communal drying rack. I turn to look at them, but then a deep, gravelly masculine voice mutters from inside the bin. It's low, irritated, and *definitely* not mine. I snap back around as it speaks words.

"Hands off my trash, pretty boy."

I freeze. That's it. I've finally snapped. Not only am I turned on by trash, but I can also *hear* it say things now. Great! And say weird things. *Pretty boy?* I stare at the bin, my eyes wide with shock and fear. I shove down the excited feeling I get.

The bin stares back.

...OK, that might be an exaggeration, but I *swear* the air around the bin had shifted or something. Or did it? Who knows, now that I know bins can speak to me, I wouldn't be surprised if they could watch me too.

I take a few slow steps back, my pulse hammering in my throat.

"I-uh-" words don't come out. My mouth is dry. My brain can't find words.

I have exactly two rational explanations for what just happened. One, my brain is finally dead from years of horny-trash-curse suppression and I'm hallucinating and hearing voices from the trash, or two, some asshole at this firm has learnt of my condition and is playing a prank on me.

Maybe some half-cocked lawyer is standing behind the shut door just waiting to mess with me. But if he's hiding there, why did I hear the voice come through, clear as day, from the trash can? Neither of these options makes me feel better. As if to make me even more rattled, I swear I see the bin shift, like it's ever so slightly adjusting itself. As it does, a protein bar wrapper falls out. Ignoring the pulse that shoots through me, I reach to pick it up.

I flinch as it speaks again.

"Did... I... stutter?"

I leave the wrapper where it lies. The voice is annoyed now. It's irritated, deep and carries the exasperation I'd expect from a man forced to deal with idiots all day.

I don't know what comes over me, but I grab the closest mop from my cart and point the wooden end at the bin. I move closer, closer, and nudge it, as if to prove to myself the voice is coming from the bin.

The voice booms again, and I nearly drop the mop in shock. "I... said... HANDS OFF!"

Most people would run. But I'm not most people and felt a little brave. Steeling myself, I clench the mop harder and brandish it like a sword.

"Listen, I don't know what kind of *Annabelle*-haunted-trash bullshit is happening here, but I *will* start swinging." I threaten, trying to make my voice as confident, deep and intimidating as possible.

Silence.

For a split second, I believe I am imagining things. The fluorescent lights even work normally again. Then, just as I convince myself the voices aren't real, the fluorescent lights shut off, and I'm plunged back to the scarily dim green exit light. The bin does a slow, deliberate movement; the lid creaks open, lifting like a clamshell. A mixture of smells floods my nostrils and then—a hand emerges, like some sort of zombie hand breaking soil out of a grave for the first time. The supernatural world being public had been great and all—I'm not a *Nuller*, anti-supernatural, but zombies in my bin is not what I signed up for!

My entire body jerks backward so fast, I trip over the wheels of my cart, crumpling down to the floor. A bottle of disinfectant also clatters down with me.

I shift up, and my eyes widen with shock as something crawls out of it.

The pale, slightly grimy hand reaches for the rim. Fingers grip around the edge, and then, it's no longer just a hand—a figure pulls itself up from inside the bin.

I see his eyes first. Sharp, amber-coloured, and glowing faintly in the dim green light. He has dark seaweed-coloured hair and is wearing a jacket that definitely looks like it's seen better days. What gets me is his skin—it's slightly see-through, glowing a green so subtle I thought it had been the exit sign reflecting off him. And I can't tell if he's slick with sweat or whatever juice that pools at the bottom of this bin, but something's dripping off the bits of skin I can see.

The next thing is the smirk; lazy and unimpressed. Like he had just sprung me sniffing the rubbish bin.

The man leans against the bin's inner rim—the angle looks impossible without tilting the bin over from the weight, but he makes it look like the most natural thing in the world. His fingers drum against the plastic rim. Is it from impatience? But what would he be impatient for?

"Weeeeell?" he says. "You gonna scream like everyone else, or can we move past the whole 'Oh no, a talking trash ghost!' bit?"

I don't scream. I just keep holding my mop like it's the only thing keeping me grounded and say the only thing that makes any sense.

"...What the *fuck?*"

Chapter 2 — The Garbage Man Cometh

I stare at the glowing man, this thing, as he crawls out of the bin. His hands are on the floor, and his legs slink out from the bin. He stands up only to sit back down on the bin lid; one leg crossed over the other.

I brandish the mop and hold my ground. The man looks between me and it. His eyes then fall on me, and he gives me a look as if *I'm* the weird one in this situation.

"Alright," I say, heart thundering through my ears. "I'm going to repeat my last question. *What the actual fuck?*"

He tilts his head, and he has a look on his face like he's thinking. He's considering something, but what?

"Would you like the short answer or the long one?"

"Short." I respond way too fast without even considering what the short could be.

"I live here." He gestures at the bin under him and smirks. "Next question."

I blink.

"You *live*–OK, no, that's not–" I push up my glasses and pinch the bridge of my nose, exhaling through my teeth. "*What are you?*"

Another smirk. "What *do* I look like?"

A homeless contortionist... I wanted to say. But I know not to judge someone based on their looks. Even if he is a ghost in a bin from god only knows what decade.

So instead of looking him dead in the eyes, I offer him the only thing I can think to say. "A fucking problem."

He lets out a low, amused hum, and then a chuckle. "That's unfair."

I look to him, and the emergency exit off to the side. *I should leave.*

This is obviously an overworked, exhaustion-induced hallucination. Maybe I had slipped in a puddle and bumped my head, and knowing my luck it was cleaning fluid and I'm currently unconsciously inhaling the fumes. Decaying. My brain finally melted. Maybe all of this is a dream.

It's the only plausible explanation. But dream-me would not be this aware of the fact that he is shirtless under that ragged coat. I bet his arms are lean, strong, smeared with faint streaks of grime, like he's been digging through the city itself.

I feel a bead of sweat run down my neck. God. Even now, my curse is trying to sabotage me.

He notices me staring. Then he flashes a big, toothy grin. "You're looking at me like I'm the *filthiest* thing you've ever seen." And I can tell he's saying filthy as if it's synonymous with sexy.

I don't play into it. "That's because you *literally* crawled out of a bin." I point to the bin under him, which he responds by uncrossing his legs. As they uncross, his quads and calves tense and flex–I do my best to ignore it. Maybe it is just a trick of the light? *Nope.* The sheen of bin juice shimmered over them and caught every ripple of muscle. I breathe slowly, trying to maintain composure.

He hums again, smiling to himself like it isn't an insult. "And yet, you can't seem to look away."

I scowl. Heat creeps up my neck, and I adjust my collar. "That's...got *nothing* to do with you. It's a–" I clamp my mouth shut. Nope. I am not explaining my humiliating personal hell to a bin ghost.

But his grin stretches; it's wicked and all-knowing. I gulp, wanting to wipe the sweat from my brow.

"Oh!" he says, eyes glinting with realisation and something else–delight, maybe? "You're *that* guy!"

I take a step back, mop still in my hand but now by my side. "What the hell is that supposed to mean? What guy?"

He stands now, half of his body phasing through the top of the bin. I hadn't realised how much of his torso had been hidden while he sat hunched over with a flannel shirt–now that he's vertical, I can see more of him. *So* much more of him. I avert my eyes–the last thing I need is my dick to get hard right now, and given there's a gorgeous man covered in trash in front of me? I'm struggling.

"You're *that* guy who gets hard over *garbage*." He says garbage long and seductively and then leans forward to inspect me. "I thought you were a rumour, a *myth*. The janitor who gets turned on by trash."

My stomach drops, and my blood runs ice cold. This is so humiliating. Who is talking about me? Why? Surely the entire non-human community has other, stranger, better things to gossip about. The idea that my name being thrown around in this manner now makes me feel sick.

He laughs. It's a friendly laugh. Which somehow makes this worse. "*Relax*. I don't judge. I mean, we all have our weird little habits."

Habit. The word pricks up my ears, and something intense runs in my blood. Anger, and maybe a little indignation.

"This isn't a habit. You think I *willingly* want to jerk it to food scraps and empty coffee cups?" I'm conflicted.

As far as he knows, how I feel about trash is my choice. A kink. It's not. I am fighting the urge not to blurt it out, but I am losing the battle between my arousal and the truth.

"I'm cursed–" The words fall out of my mouth faster than I can stop myself. I snap my mouth shut.

But it's too late. His expression sharpens, intrigued. "Oh?" he goes to continue, but whatever words he had formed die on his tongue as his eyes land down at my waist.

I follow his line of sight and can see, and feel, that I am rock hard. The tension pulses against the material of my janitor overalls. As if one flex would rip a hole through it.

Shit!

I try to hide it with the broom, but, well... the handle is *definitely* not adequate. Like a strand of hay blocking a power pole.

His grin stretches wider, staring at my bulging crotch as I stand there blushing. "Now *that* is interesting."

I stand frozen, my face in flames. Despite my embarrassment, my dick seems to have a mind of its own; in fact, it seems to only get harder with each passing second.

His grin stretches wider, sharp canine teeth peeking out like he's just been handed the most interesting piece of gossip. He phases through the bin entirely, sits back down on the lid and looks me up and down, and the way his eyes trail over me, it's like he sees me as this fascinating puzzle he needs to put together.

The non-cursed me would be freaked out and already running away. But my cursed form is pulling me to him like a magnet. I am in a tug of war between what is right, what is decent, and wanting to fuck the shit out of this trash ghost. Which wouldn't be decent. But it would be a good time and exactly what my dick was begging for as it flexed again.

"You weren't kidding," he murmurs. I hate how pleased he sounds. "That's quite the... err, *reaction*."

My pulse is fast; it thumps in my ears like a drumbeat. And my dick flexes with desire, begging me to relieve it. I push away the thought, but that seems to make it ache more. *The fucking thing has a mind of its own!*

He moves closer. I say, "Don't," but it's quieter than I intend.

"Don't *what*?" his voice drips with amusement. "I'm just standing here, minding my business. You're the one getting worked up over a trashcan." He points between his legs.

I catch myself licking my lips. I stop and let out a heavy breath. He looks back up at me.

"Kinda seems like a *you* problem."

I'm sweating. I clench my jaw, gripping the broom tight like it might save me from this train-wreck of a shift. "This–this isn't–"

His bright amber eyes gleam at me. "You said it was a curse."

The rest of my body stiffens now. "So what if I did?"

He hums, tilting his head. He's studying me, and I feel like I'm under a microscope. "Then I have bad news for you, Janitor Boy."

Before I can tell him not to call me that, my name badge is *right* there, he walks forward and leans in. His voice drops to something almost intimate. "Curses don't just happen." He phases his hand through my overalls at the waist and runs his fingers up. I look down but can't feel his fingers, but I can feel a sensation like an echo of wet silk dragging along my skin. Mixed with his pungent yet sweet odour of rotting banana and used tea bags, mixed with a less discernible odour of leather and sweat that fills my nostrils, my balls tighten into my stomach and the head of my cock swells.

"They come with conditions." He continues. And I wish he wouldn't. The longer I stand here, smelling him, looking at the bits of his glistening body I can see peeking out under that coat, the more I just want to pull my cock out of my janitor suit and cover the walls in cum.

"There are rules. A trigger. There are loopholes too." He pauses and watches my face carefully. I perk up at the loophole, and he seems to notice that. He's testing a theory. "Something tells me you've never tried to break it... *properly*."

My breath catches. I *have* tried. Five years of searching. Wasting money on fraud mystics, combing through cursed forums, getting laughed out of bogus magic shops for asking if they could fix me. Every single one told me the same thing: *There's nothing to be done. No cure. No solution.*

He watches me, and the realisation hits me; his smirk, the look on his face, it's not judgement, it's recognition. Understanding. We both know what the other is thinking. He knows I am cursed, because he must be too. No ghost just dwells in a bin, even in this supernatural-friendly world.

"Yeah," he says, smug. "That's what I thought."

I blink. Just before the curse settles in on me, I come to my senses. This is a freaking *ghost*, not just something my curse deems as an object of lust manifested. Ghosts are horrifying things, and as that thought fills my brain, my fight–or–flight instinct kicks in.

Fight? Not an option. I have never laid a hand on another man, let alone kissed one or slept with one, since the curse. So that leaves me with the other option.

Flight. Yes. That! AND NOW!

I drop the mop and spin on my heel. I rip the door open behind me and flee down the hallway, turning immediately left, not worrying about the concerned looks on the faces of lawyers as I sprint past them.

"Hey!" his voice is distant, but I can hear him call after me. It's rich in laughter. "Running won't fix your trash problem, handsome!"

I just run. My feet take me out of the building through the fire escape; I'm on the street, and everything's too much. I duck into an alleyway nearby and catch my breath, my chest heaving as I lean against the brick wall, the cool air outside calming my nervous system.

Whatever this bin–haunting bastard had planned, the non-cursed part of me didn't want to wait around and find out.

What would people say next? He's moved from trash to *ghosts*. I couldn't bear the embarrassment.

Chapter 3—Trash Will Find You

I had been prepared to write yesterday off as a delusion of my tired mind–until I was called in early and couldn't stop thinking about it.

About *him*.

The office is cool, crisp with recycled air and the faint scent of overpriced coffee.

I am already sweating bullets. Not because of the temperature building inside the restricting janitor's uniform. Not because I am out of shape either.

I am actually in fantastic shape. Working out helps me keep my perversity at bay–it's a great distraction. But no, I am sweating because a huge part of me knows whatever happened wasn't imaginary and he's here.

Somewhere.

Waiting.

Lurking in a bin.

I grip the handle of my cleaning cart so tight that if I somehow could grip it harder, it would bond with my skin. My shoulders are tense as I push the cart out into the office. With a deep sigh, I lift them to my ears and drop them, forcing them to relax.

This is just another shift.

Just. Get. Through. This shift.

This is a totally *normal* and *completely* non-haunted shift, surrounded by corporate living human types who will absolutely not appreciate if I scream at a bin.

Or worse. Fuck it.

I shake my head at the thought of the CEO of Graves & Pennington LLP walking in on me getting it on with the bin and looking horrified.

"Morning," a passing accountant mumbles, barely looking up from their phone and heading towards the lift upstairs.

"Good morning," I say, attempting to sound cheerful while resisting the urge to knock their phone out their hands and grab them by the shoulders and ask *If you could see a trash spirit in a bin, you'd tell me, right?*

The lights hum overhead as I push my cart toward the supply closet. The office is pretty quiet, except for the clacking of keyboards and inane office murmur. I eye every bin I pass as if he will pop out from any of them at any moment. Every discarded takeaway coffee cup taunts me. Every crumbled food wrapper. I feel beads of sweat trickle down my back. At least I don't have to worry about sweat stains-the janitor uniform is dark.

As if to dispel my thoughts and anxieties, I shake my head and push the cart forward, locking my gaze ahead. The squeak of my cart's rolling wheels scratches through the air of the office, setting me further on edge. Like the countdown theme song from Jaws.

But as I round the corner toward the kitchen, I hear him.

His voice. Low. Smug. Like he is whispering in my ear.

"Miss me, Janitor Boy?"

My breath catches, and I pull the cart to a sharp halt, knocking over some supplies.

I whip around, heart hammering.

Nothing. Nobody was there.

The hallway is empty. The office workers are all at their desks. Nothing's around me except the small waste bin along the wall between the cabinets. It sits innocently against the wall. But I know it's not.

I back away slowly, my heart practically pounding through my ribcage. *Just ignore it... him. Keep moving.*

I tentatively keep walking. The lights above me flicker once... then again. I stop in my tracks. The bin-man is playing with me now, and a chill runs down my spine, making me shudder.

Flight's kicking in again. Abandoning my cart, I rush past the bin and towards the door marked 'Janitor's Office'.

Safety.

My hand flies to the handle, and I grip it. Behind me, I hear a soft, eerie chuckle. I shake my head and shut my eyes. I'm hallucinating again. Or maybe I'm on drugs-*I shouldn't have trusted that donut Claudia gave me this morning*. Wait, maybe Claudia's playing a prank on me...maybe she is behind all of this. She does like to taunt me. It is our friendship love language. And let's face it, if you don't gently bully your friends, are they really your friends?

I ignore the voice and twist the handle. I push the door open, and my heart drops. There he is. Sitting there with a smirk, he's in the only bin in the office. It's impossibly small, and I don't know how he fits inside it. He's resting his elbows on the lip of the bin, his chin in his hands. As he notices me, my heart races and my eyes bulge from the shock of seeing him again.

I hope for footsteps behind me, for someone else to witness what I am witnessing. He leans back, arms behind his head as if he were on a damn beach holiday taking in the warm sun.

He is dressed exactly the same as in our last encounter. The same sheen of bin juice on his chest. The black singlet with a flannel over top.

"'Bout time!" he says, in what I think is a provoking tone. "I was beginning to miss that gorgeous face behind those slutty wire-frame glasses!"

I quickly rush inside and shut the door behind me, careful not to let it slam to disturb everyone in the office. As I turn, I speak in a sharp whisper. "What are you doing here?"

He just shrugs and then grins widely at me. "So *skittish*. We had some unfinished business. Thought I would pop on by over to this bin, though it is far more cramped than my favourite in the kitchen."

He can move between bins! Great! I groan internally. No escape.

He seems to realise I've made this discovery, and he grins wider. Were these bins some sort of interconnected portals?

"You can't just show up wherever you want. There are people here!"

"Oh? Them?" He smirked once more. He needed to stop doing that... I felt a flexing in my pants again. *Fuck's sake!*

"None of them can see me, Oscar." He adds. At first, I had been shocked he knew my name, but then I remembered my name is stitched to the chest of my janitor's overalls.

I thought that would have frustrated me. But it brought me relief. If nobody else can see him, then he's *clearly* not real, and I truly am just having delusions of grandeur. There's relief knowing he will probably go away with some sleep, or caffeine, or anti-psychotics, or something else.

I might as well entertain myself with this hallucination.

"You said it was a curse," he murmured.

Not this again.

"What if I tell you I have a solution?"

My ears prick up. Words fall out of my mouth. "What do you mean?"

He leaned back against the rim of the bin. "I've been around a long time, Handsome. I've seen a lot of weird shit. Get all sorts of items dumped through my head daily. But yours didn't even make the top ten in the '*Big Bad Book of Curses To*

Mess With Humans' Lives'." He licked his thumb and pre-tended to turn a page in a book.

Handsome. He called me handsome. Guys have called me attractive in the past, or good-looking, but never hand-some. Handsome is a word I reserve for someone I really like. He used *my* word. My heart wants to swell.

Instead, my head swirls with questions, of which I didn't want to know the answers. Questions about all the shit he has seen.

He grins again. He needs to stop grinning...

"It is triggered by trash. But a triggered curse is one that can be broken, by what sets it off."

This didn't make sense...

I had been caught by coworkers in the past when the curse activated and I had jerked into an empty takeaway coffee cup. And again, when I fucked a turkey sandwich. The urge never goes away. If anything, I just find something new. I wanted to correct him, but he had to be an expert on this. I mean, look at *him*!

I can't wipe the look of befuddlement off my face.

"You obviously wouldn't know that though. I have been watching you for a while. You let no one help you." He pushes himself up and appears to be standing within the bin. "In fact, I wager you have never truly let anyone help you do anything before."

I stare at him, and my voice catches in my throat. I want to scream at him. Squirt every drop of cleaning liquid at him. Tie up the bag and chuck it outside. But I knew it wouldn't work. If he could appear here, it would be more than likely the bins outside are connected too.

"Didn't think so, handsome." He smirks. That damn word again. "Lucky for you, I am in a helpful mood."

What did that even mean?

He smiles even wider at me, looking sweaty and nervous. *Nervous about what?* "If we are to do this, there is something I should tell you first–"

The janitor's office door flies open behind me, and I turn around, fear in my eyes.

"Hey, Oscar? You in? There's been a spill–"

It's Claudia. She stops, eyes wide, sees me, then looks to the bin behind me, and I look back and hope he isn't there.

And he isn't. *Thank fuck! The Bin-man is gone.* But I have to be hallucinating. I blink a few times. He still isn't there.

All she can see is me, standing alone in a cramped janitor's office, my glasses slipping down my nose. I push them back up and pretend like nothing is happening.

"...You, OK?" she asks, genuine care in her tone. "Who were you talking to?"

If this had been a prank she is pulling, she is doing a damn good job at acting. I decide to play along. "Yeah!" my voice squeaks. "Just, uh," I look around and quickly grab a few bottles of bleach. "Just reorganising the um, cleaning supplies. Sometimes it helps me to say them out loud."

She gives me a look that makes it clear she's not convinced. And at this point, I realise she isn't pulling a prank and has nothing to do with Bin-man.

"OK, well once you are done doing whatever it is you were doing, can you come clean up the spill in the lift foyer?"

She leaves, shutting the door behind her. I can catch my breath. I press my forehead against the wall and let go of the bleach bottles.

What the fuck is wrong with me? Why is this happening to me?

I hear a voice. At first, I think it's from somewhere above me, but then I eye the bin. As I peer down into it, a pair of glistening amber eyes look back from deep within it, as if from another realm. I hear his voice once again.

"Running won't fix your trash problem, handsome, but maybe you could try kissing me? What have you got to lose?"

He has to be kidding. He isn't even real, just a figment of my imagination. I pull myself together and gather what I need and then leave.

Of course, my cursed mind would create a man who got me hot and bothered that only I could see. The feeling stung sharper than a slap. I was never lucky in love. And this felt worse than that disastrous date I went on many years ago that had turned into the craziest six weeks of my life. I had no actual evidence, but I *know* my witch-of-an-ex is the one who cursed me. He promised he would make me pay for leaving him. Just picturing him sends a chill through me, like I can still hear him growling about revenge.

I hear a whisper follow me, just before I shut the door behind me.

"Trash will find you."

Chapter 4—Binfluencer

I get through the rest of my shift by avoiding the kitchen and my coworkers, and I one thousand percent avoid any contact with trash, bins or any empty mugs, in case I spontaneously ejaculate all over the damn place. I don't know what I'd do if he were to appear again and offer to kiss me. Hell, I don't know what I'd do if he calls me handsome again; I'd rather not find out.

Although avoiding the problem had proven to be difficult when I am the only janitor rostered for the entire building. I keep myself busy doing small, odd jobs around the office, fixing some light bulbs, reporting a broken air vent and even mopping up that mess in the front foyer area that Claudia wanted me to.

I had avoided further encounters with the bin-man. Being outed again for my trash kink-sorry, curse-is not on my agenda to repeat for today. Nor is running out of the building from the shame. I'm not repeating yesterday twice. *This is what we call progress, people!*

I had shaken off the mixed feelings of horniness meets shame meets fear of a ghost man coming out of a bin entirely. My shift's getting close to being over - I think I can survive the rest of the day. I'm feeling confident, even though I am in the executive bathroom right now restocking the toilet rolls; some would say this isn't good, but to me this is far better than taking out the bins right now.

As I finish up and leave, I hear the familiar clacking noise of stilettos behind me as I reach the foyer. I spin around. It's Claudia.

"Oh, there you are." She looks spooked. "I thought I was going crazy before when I walked into the closet with you there."

I blink and almost gulp. Claudia's my only friend here, and though she doesn't know my full secret, I have told her about most of my sex life failures. Maybe it is time to let her in on this too?

"Oh, did you see the man standing in the bin as well?"

She pauses and looks at me like I'm crazy. "What? No... but I got such a migraine-inducing energy blast as I walked past that room again. A full-body shiver, third eye aching." She rubs her temples.

I fumble a replacement toilet roll, and it lands on the floor, rolling to the other side of the room, bouncing off her shoe. My heart skips. I'm relieved. She didn't see the bin-man, but now I am confused, more than ever. "Energy blast?" I ask her.

She shrugs and casually states that she is sort-of-psychic, as if it were a normal everyday thing. I go to laugh, because, what the fuck? But who am I to judge? I have a freaking trash kink curse, and I'm hallucinating a bin ghost man. Anything's possible.

She notices that I'm stifling a reaction to her revelation, but she continues to talk like it's the same as announcing something inane like she changed coffee shops. "I am on the low sensitivity scale, trust me I have been tested. I'm sort of like a spiritual Wi-Fi extender." She taps her temple.

Tested? Wh... what?

She continues. "I mostly feel vibes. I have occasionally seen ghosts, or what I *suspect* are ghosts. One time I channelled a dead pigeon, and the heartbreak I felt made me coo-sob into the cinnamon scroll I was eating."

"...OK." It's all I can say as we both sit on a bench in the foyer. "So, why are you telling me all this? Not that I don't believe you, it's just..." I shrug.

"I'm telling you this because you look like you've seen a ghost. Or something worse, like you got railed by one."

My entire face ignites, and I stammer out my response. "I have not—he didn't—that's not what happened!"

I cover my mouth and look at her with what I think are dinner plates for eyes. Claudia narrows hers. "Oscar." She says gently, pausing for a few seconds. "You've been acting odd. Odder than usual. You know I love you, but I've seen you talk to yourself. I see you flinch at bins, and the other day you wouldn't take my smashed coffee cup to the kitchen." She points down the hall, and I look and swallow hard, wiping my brow with my forearm.

"And you're sweating like you just ran a marathon through a haunted landfill."

So... *specific*. As usual. I say nothing but look guilty.

She shuffles closer, and the quietness between us is palpable. It is that trusted quietness between friends. I could sit with Claudia and just exist; she always makes me feel comfortable. She never judges me. So, I decide now is the right time to explain my predicament.

"I think." I start and then shake my head. "No, I *know* I'm cursed. I've been for years. Looking at trash causes me to... uh."

"Get aroused?"

It's poised like a question, but she says it like she knows she's right. Which...She is. Now that I know she's sort of psychic, all of those odd questions she sometimes asks me now make sense. "Yes." I hang my head.

"Well, we all have our proclivities. You could find much worse things attractive. Actually..." she paused and held onto my hand, stroking it with her thumb. "You're a *janitor*. I'm sure it makes your job hard... no pun intended."

We share a laugh at the irony. And it's welcome–it dispels the worry I had about her reaction. I've not exactly had great experiences telling people about this part of me.

Claudia's face turns a little sombre as the joke dies down. "If you don't mind my asking, how did it happen?"

"That part I don't know for certain, but I suspect it was my witchy ex who's hell-bent on revenge for dumping him." I lied at the end. I didn't want to say it was he who dumped me. Or the reason.

"Gay men can be so petty, especially witches."

We pause, and then she presses me about what has been going on in the office. I tell her about the first encounter with the bin-man yesterday, and today's visit too.

"Whatever is following you in the office... it isn't malevolent."

I arch an eyebrow. "How do you know?"

"Just the vibe I am getting. He sounds powerful, and hot too... like some sort of bin ghost thirst trapping Adonis. And as if he asked you to kiss him!"

She makes him sound so delectable. Desirable. Like I said, she never makes me feel like I'm being judged.

"He is pretty cute. If ghosts had the internet, he absolutely would be a *Binfluencer*."

Claudia snorts, and it makes me laugh along with her. "I don't judge, but if your spectral boyfriend wants to manifest again and spend time with you, I say give him a chance. After all, you could do a lot worse. The men of the mortal realm are all bumbling, incompetent fools and lack any awareness of how unfunny they are and how utterly useless in bed they are."

I nod numbly. *Yes, they are.*

The day passes uneventfully, and I finish my shift without a hitch.

In the locker room where I change in and out of my janitor uniform, I glimpse myself in the mirror. My hair is a mess, my glasses are grimy, and my face is flushed.

All day, I've done nothing but think of him.

This curse has wrecked my life. It's cost me jobs and ruined any prospects of a relationship. It stains my dignity beyond anything bleach could remove.

But today?

I find myself smiling stupidly. For the first time in five years, someone finally said they might understand it. Might even fix it.

Even if that someone is a bin-haunting, smirking chaos spirit who thinks I am *handsome*. The word rattles in my brain as I slip into my casual clothes. I walk out of the locker room and into the office again. Everyone had gone for the day, and it is just me, alone.

Across the room, the janitor's closet creaks open, and my heart flutters. *What the hell, even my pants tighten!* Like a salivating dog from a Pavlovian response.

A familiar voice purrs, and that makes me smile. "I told you trash will find you."

And there he is.

He's out of his bin and standing on the floor. His bare legs, shiny with bin juice, are exposed from the jean shorts he wore, and this time he wasn't wearing his flannel overshirt. His bin-juice-soaked boots leave stains on the carpet. A normal janitor would be livid, but me? I am nothing but an animal in heat at the sight of it. *Of him.*

The grin on his face spreads like an oil spill. His form flickers–he is no longer the completely translucent form he had been during the day. He is exactly how he had been when I first saw him. Not quite solid. Not quite ghostly.

Half a man. Half a trashy mess. And oh, so fuckable. Covered in bin juice. How is it possible that a spirit, man, whatever, dwelling in the bin has me so frazzled?

Fuck, I want this man more than I even know. My dick definitely does too; I can feel it pulsing and flexing, daring to push through my jeans. I shudder as it rubs up against the zipper.

Yes, I go commando. Ever since I had been cursed, I had gone through too many pairs of underwear and hadn't really had time to keep up with my washing. So I just went without one day and never turned back.

"Ready to break that curse?" he asks, his eyes fluttering at me, coaxing me inside the janitor's closet.

And just like that, I think I am saying yes. My feet are at least. They lead my body, boner first, towards this man, who I am probably about to fuck, and who I don't even know his name.

Standard gay experience.

Before I know it, I am inside the office again, door shut, heart racing, dick throbbing and my brain swirling.

Chapter 5—Bin Cursed

There are so many reasons I shouldn't agree to sleeping with this ghost.

Reason one: he is literally a bin-dwelling spirit man.

Reason two: he is, without a doubt, the most insufferable, smug cunt I have ever met.

Reason three: I cannot control my erection around him.

Reason four: The *curse* would be sleeping with him, not *me*, and that makes me feel disgusting.

Reason five: I literally melt when he calls me Janitor Boy or Handsome. And–nope. I don't have the time or the strength anymore for those kinds of feelings.

But ultimately none of these reasons matter. As I stack them up, the rational side of my trash-and-dickmatised brain gives a counterargument I can't refuse or argue my way out of. I need this curse to be broken. Maybe a therapist too. Probably both.

But, how can I break the curse when I can't even say anything to him?

Here I am, sitting across from him in the janitor's closet, blanketed by fluorescent lights. He had joined me, sitting on the floor. His legs are crossed, resting on his boots. They're a pair of grimy, steel-capped workers boots, but through the grime and muck I can make out a faint tan colour. The kind tradies would wear.

The bin behind him had not yet been emptied by me–I planned on dealing with it tomorrow. I push down the thoughts of me sticking *something* in the trashcan. Right now, I need to deal with this, whatever *this* is.

I can't handle our silence. It's the most uncomfortable silence between two people–sorry, one person and one spirit–who are one hundred percent not on a date.

This is not a date; I keep telling myself. We're just... hanging out.

We had talked at length about what specifically triggered my curse. When I told him that all forms of trash did, it had me fucked up. Because how can you tell someone what turns you on when that someone also turns you on? He's the manifestation of the perfect bin-juice scented sex doll I could ever dream of.

"So..." he says, his eyes focusing on me, like he's trying to see more of me. "How did it occur?"

Déjà vu. My conversation with Claudia comes to mind, but I dismiss the thought. "I figure it was my witchy ex and his funny way of getting revenge."

Silence. Then, he bursts out laughing–a genuine belly laugh.

"OK, wow. Fuckin' relatable. What did you do to your ex to deserve this?"

I wince, and my brow furrows. "Nothing. Don't laugh; it's not funny."

"It kind of is. Must have been something big for him to do this to you."

I shake my head. "He said I didn't value him. Said I treated him like garbage. Said he would make me finally respect the discarded objects of the world."

He inspects me. He sees me, and that brief flick of validation and genuine interest in me makes words fall out.

"So now my body—well mostly my dick—reacts to trash. The worse it smells and looks, the harder I get."

He looks at himself–the grime covering his skin and looks back at me with a grin. "I must be a walking filthy sex doll for you then or something, ha-ha!"

He laughs, obviously joking around, but little does he know...

I changed the subject. "I would rather not think about that right now."

He doesn't skip a beat. His eyes trail down me, and he chuckles. "You might not, but *he* is positively about to burst through your pants." He points at my crotch, and I look down. My throbbing erection flexes upward.

I shove it down with my hands and try to think of something else. I change the topic, again.

"So, you're a...?"

"A Grouch," he instantly says back to me. "For the longest time, I didn't remember my name. It was *discarded* along with my corporeal body when I passed over."

My stomach rumbles, making him laugh. And my hard-on still hasn't gone down. My eyes flick over to a nearby cupboard. Good, I have an idea. "I haven't eaten all day. Do you mind if I make something?"

"Go right ahead."

I head to the cupboard, grab a pack of instant noodles, and head to the office's kitchen. I leave these at work for shifts where I am stuck behind cleaning and don't make it back to my apartment in time for proper dinner. Being away from him also helps my cock go down to a softer semi.

Using the filtered hot water faucet, I stir the cup with more force than necessary, and some of the boiling broth spills over the lip. I shake my hand as the burning liquid drops on me and head back to him, where he awaits, slightly happy to see me return.

"So, how exactly does this deal work?" I ask as I swirl some noodles on my fork and take in a mouthful.

His gaze falls to his lap. "Simple. We know your trigger. Now we shut it down. You'll stop getting hot over trash, and I—"

He looks up, and he finally meets my gaze, and something in his smirk wavers for just a second. "I stop being what I am."

I pause, fork mid-air. "You stop being a Grouch?"

He shrugs way too casually, as if he didn't just wish to stop existing. "Maybe?" he says simply. "I have never really done this before, only heard about it from others who..." he pauses, his eyes glistening. "I don't see anymore... Either way, I get to help someone out in dire need, and I also get to step out of the bin for more than a few hours at a time."

Oh, so it doesn't cause him to stop existing. He just gains freedom. "Is that something you want?"

He tilts his head and answers in a way that completely stumps me. "Would *you* want to live for an eternity defined by what everyone else threw away?"

He leans forward, and I bump my noodle cup, gasping slightly as boiling water pours over my thumb again.

"Ah!" It stings, and I pull back, but The Grouch pulls my hand toward him in a way I can't even fathom. He is translucent and see-through but also not. Like a poltergeist, but not as annoying.

He blows on it, and that cools it down almost instantly. "So, enough about me, let's go back to *you*."

"I'd rather we didn't" I turn away from him, but he pulls me back by the chin with his finger. Surprisingly, my dick doesn't twitch, and for a moment I think I may have been cured, but then my curse activates, and it flexes in my pants once again. I do my best to ignore it.

"Come on. You can trust me. What was the first memory you have of the curse being triggered?"

I groan, which only makes him grin at me. You'd think that a man who dwells in a bin would have rotten teeth, but his were pure white.

"I don't know if I can say it... it's so embarrassing." I say. He gives me a look that urges me on. "OK, fine... it was a sandwich." And my cheeks flush bright red.

He perks up. "What kind?"

"Does it matter?"

"Yes!" He is way too eager to know more. "I need to know what type of trash your type is. We're building a profile here."

I bury my face in my hands.

"You are so fucking cute when you are embarrassed, do you know that?"

Thank fuck I had already felt embarrassed, because now he will never know my cheeks are blushing because he called me cute. And not *just* cute, *but fucking* cute.

I look up and peer between my fingers. "It was a turkey and cranberry baguette."

Without a beat, he whistles. "Great choice!"

In this moment, I want the floor to open and swallow me whole, but something compels me to continue. Like I'm possessed to tell him more.

"It even had a little toothpick flag. I... uhhh... kept it."

"Oh, my!" He looks at me with sheer delight. "You are worse than I thought."

"Weren't we meant to be finding out how to shut the trigger down?" I beg.

And as if I offended him, he pulls back and scoffs. "Fine." He then smiles again. "We need to perform some experiments."

"Experiments?"

He leans forward again; eyes glistening and licks his lips. He is clearly enjoying this.

"I think I know a way that could stop it. But it involves you giving in to your desires. Trust me, I won't ask you to kiss me again; there are other things to test."

There's a quick sense of relief I feel. Because I know damn well if he asked me to kiss him, I don't think I would have stopped him. But my ears wilt at 'other things'. And if it involves doing what I did to that baguette, hell no. I have only ever done that in the privacy of my apartment, especially not involving anyone.

OK, besides all the times I had been caught at other jobs when the curse-arousal took over.

When I was literally fucking a discarded ham and cheese sandwich, using the leftover mayo as lube to glide through the... I shake my head. I need to stop thinking about it.

But besides that, I have been careful not to bring anyone into my drama. And here is a solution handed to me on a trash-covered platter, and I am hesitant. I wish I could allow myself to let people help me instead of pushing them away.

But I've been cursed for years now. Nothing I've done myself has worked. I need his help more than I care to admit.

The conversation continues, and we arrange to meet back here on the weekend when there would be no risk of being caught by coworkers. He leaves the logistics to me. Which now means I need an excuse to come here on the weekend, of which I'm not usually rostered on because the office shuts then.

Today being Thursday means tomorrow is Friday, and Saturday comes afterwards. *Thanks, Rebecca Black, for confirming that for an entire generation.* It gave me a day to figure it all out. Just one day... what could go wrong?

Chapter 6—Can't Refuse Him

I spend most of Friday morning trying to figure out how to tell my boss that I am required to come in on the weekend. I obviously have to omit that it is for deeply cursed reasons, but I need something real to use.

Fridays used to bring me joy. They were normally full of hopeful sips of my coffee, always in a travel cup and instantly washed up so I wouldn't be tempting my own fate, and the glimmer that the week is nearly over.

But this Friday?

Mine begins with my fake laughing at Claudia's joke about ghosts in the photocopier while crafting a full-blown, morally dubious lie in my head. A lie about why I *need* to be in the office tomorrow.

The problem with lying? You must keep up the charade and remember who you have told, what you have told, and all the details. When I got cursed, after the first couple of times of being caught fucking a coffee cup stuffed with a sandwich or cheesecake, as if it were some sort of depraved discarded fleshjack, I had developed a method of keeping up with the lies.

Keep them simple and effective. I need to figure out something that would obviously be in my wheelhouse of tasks but not too specific or out of the ordinary that I would be questioned.

Claudia's some sort of walking Bluetooth lie detector - probably tied to her being a psychic - because she sees right through me. She's sipping her turmeric latte, waiting for her

photocopying to finish, and eyes me with what I think is
suspicious serenity. I feel beads of sweat forming on my
forehead. She narrows her eyes as if she can smell my panic.
Knowing her, she probably *could*.

I keep my tone breezy, like my internal monologue
isn't full of a Shakespearean tragic soliloquy:

O CRUEL ENCHANTMENT! O MOST VILE AFFLICTION! THAT I, BORN WITH
NEITHER GRANDEUR NOR GLORY, SHOULD BE SO WICKEDLY UNDONE BY
WASTE!

WHAT SIN DID I COMMIT, WHAT BIN DID I OFFEND? THAT NOW I STAND
-A MAN, YET LESS THAN MAN- STIRRED BY GREASE-STAINED
WRAPPERS AND SOILED FOAM CUPS, MY PULSE QUICKENED NOT BY
LOVE, NOR LUST, BUT BY THE SCENT OF TRASH LONG LEFT TO ROT.

EACH RUBBISH HEAP BECOMES A SIREN'S SONG, EACH CRUMPLED
RECEIPT A LOVE LETTER TO MY UNDOING!

AND LO! THE GHOST-THE GROUCH, THAT CURSED WRETCH WITH EYES
LIKE FLAME, WHO DWELLS WITHIN MY FILTH AND MOCKS MY SHAME-HE
SMILES, AND I DO TREMBLE.

HE BECKONS, AND I OBEY.

I CAN'T REFUSE HIM, NOR ARE MY INTENTIONS.

BUT IS THIS MY FATE? TO FALL FOR THAT WHICH ALL REJECT?

TO FIND MY HEART NOT IN THE ARMS OF MEN, BUT IN A ROTTING
COMPOST BIN? SPEAK, GODS OF SANITATION!

DELIVER ME!

OR, FAILING THAT- LET THE MOP STRIKE TRUE AND END ME NOW.

"So... I'm probably coming in tomorrow," I say, pretending to look at my cleaning roster on my phone. "Do a
little extra detailing. The carpets need a steam."

Claudia blinks, and without missing a moment,
smirks. She takes another sip of her latte. "You've *never* done
extra detailing. You barely detail the things you're paid to
clean during the week..."

Damn it. She's right. This is fair. I internalise a chuckle and put my phone in my pocket to wipe the sweat off my brow. I am nervous. And I don't know why. Claudia likes me, knows about the curse and The Grouch, and is truly my only friend in this place. She's probably the only reason I still have a job here too.

No—I need to keep her out of it. It's one thing to know about my affliction, another to know that I'm going to hang around outside of hours to experiment on it with a bin ghost. I'm sure there's some kind of HR liability there...

"Well," I stammer, doubling down on the lie, "we have that event next week with the heads of corporate attending, so I want to ensure the office is spotless."

"I thought that was the weekend after this one?" Claudia adds and smirks again to herself as she drinks more of her coffee. The photocopier beeps, and she presses a button, causing more things to start printing and scanning.

She taps away at her phone. She hits a final key dramatically and then snatches whatever she had photocopied from the machine. I lean back.

"You're lying." She finally says, walking to her desk. I follow behind her as she continues. "You're going to have to be a bit more convincing if you're going to request a weekend pass. There's only one reason you would stay here late—well, there are heaps, but only one makes sense given what you said yesterday—is it a date with your bin-man?"

"What? No! It's not a date!" My voice cracks like a hot glass being run under cold water. "I just need to spend some time with the floors...and the bins...alone."

I groan. Why did I say that last bit?

She twists on the spot and gives me a look that is part psychic medium, part office gossip gremlin. "Alright, Oscar. I won't press. But if you die mysteriously after hours or I find your body stuffed in a bin... I'll find your ghost and tell you *I told you so.*"

"Noted," I mumble back. I can feel the warmth on my face; my cheeks are so flushed.

"Far out. I hope I don't come into work on Monday and you've got a water bottle stuck on your dick. Look, here, take this." She reaches for a sheet of paper on her desk, scribbles something on it, then hands it to me.

"What's this?" I ask, turning it around and looking at the form.

"It's an extra cleaning request signed off by me. Henry will not even think about it if I ask him for it. Especially if I suddenly have turmeric latte stains all over my cubicle's carpet, which could take days to clean if it sets in..."

Without missing a beat, she takes the lid off her coffee and pours it. I panic for a second, looking around, but nobody notices her do it. The yellow liquid quickly seeps into her cream-coloured cubicle carpet, and for the first time ever, I'm genuinely happy to see a mess. She's smiling at me. I appreciate Claudia's friendship and her wing woman behaviours. She wants the best for me and ensured that it happened.

She pats me on the shoulder and leans forward to whisper. "Tell me all the sordid details on Monday." she winks.

I thank her and scuttle off to continue my rounds, heart hammering. I immediately walk to Henry's office, the HR officer, and knock on his door.

Henry's a middle-aged man who told me he once dreamed of being a detective but settled for Human Resources because here, he is a bigger fish in this pond. He has a permanent scowl etched on his face, not from anger but from administrative fatigue.

His salt-and-pepper beard is trimmed to his own self-imposed regulated stuffy corporate guy length of which I have never seen it grow any longer; his glasses are perched on his forehead, and an open page of the newspaper on his desk has a sudoku puzzle waiting for him to finish it. His office smells faintly of instant coffee and overly citrusy hand sanitizer.

I always say to Claudia that despite his overly stiff professionalism and a demeanour like a metal scouring pad that you just know he once owned a mug that had the words *It's not an argument. I'm just telling you why I am right*.

A singular gruff, followed by "Enter!" signals me in.

I turn the handle and walk in.

"Oh, Oscar, just the man I wanted to see. We are having a delivery tomorrow, and no one is available to come in. You wouldn't be free at all?"

All that work, just so I'd be handed an excuse to come in. Far out. The universe works in mysterious ways. "Uh, actually, yeah, I am free!" I started trying to play it cool. "I was already planning on coming in over the weekend, so this works out great. Claudia requested an extra cleaning job that would take a couple of days to do." I hand him the form, and he snatches it without looking at me. As he reads, his glasses drop to the bridge of his nose.

"Well, this all looks in order. You OK with handling a delivery?" His tone felt condescending.

"*Yes*, just tell me where it needs to go." I reply with a bit of snark he doesn't pick up on. *Why are straight men always so oblivious to good sarcastic humour?*

"Thanks for this. So, the delivery is set for nine, but they sometimes get here early. Give me a buzz when it's all done, won't you? Then you can get to that coffee stain for Claudia."

"Sure will." I say, and I leave his office and shut the door. I could have danced towards my janitor's closet from how excited I am that my plans are working out.

Chapter 7—So Binto you

B y the time the afternoon rolls around, I am running on fumes, anxiety and the haunting echoes of The Grouch's voice whispering "curse-breaking weekend" to me like it is fore-play.

I have one more task left before I can clock off: a blitz stock-up of all the amenities around the office just in case we make a mess. There is something about getting a job done and done well that feels sacred. It's a benediction of bleach and overused mops.

Everyone has already left for the evening, and I am doing my last sweep around with the quiet reverence of a man preparing to do something stupid.

It's not a date. I keep reiterating this to myself. I can't fall for this spirit. He is going to help me break my curse, and then we are going to go our separate ways. A casual meetup with a bin spirit. *Totally normal.*

My cart squeaks mournfully as I pull it along behind me. The wheels are acting like they are against the whole idea and warning me not to go through with it. But it is too late. I've signed the paperwork and gotten the go-ahead from HR, Claudia knows, and even implicated herself in my plans with the turmeric stains on her carpet. *I can't forget to actually clean it.*

The wink she gave me too, like she is a proud high schooler winking to her friend who was about to lose their v-card at prom. She isn't exactly wrong. My v-card is long gone, but I have a feeling someone's going to get railed.

I had almost finished all my tasks. Scrapping the weird red stain off someone's desk, that suspiciously looked like blood but had the texture of protein smoothie, emptied all the bins, and even getting the weird grey goo off the carpet near Finance. I am in every professional sense at the pinnacle of janitorial excellence.

So why does my hand shake as I grip the mop?

I push open the kitchenette door. It is dark, with just the faint green exit sign humming like a whisper. The three bins sat in their usual corner. This had been where it all began.

I hesitantly lift the lid and peer inside. It's empty. My heart sank. I had hoped to see him again before our rendezvous, but I guess it's fine not to see him.

"Thought I'd find you here!"

I scream like an absolute banshee, clutching the mop as a weapon once again. The Grouch stands nearby, leaning against a vending machine, arms crossed. The smug bin-born grin curls like cigarette smoke across his face.

He looks a lot more solid tonight - the greenish translucent hue that's normally around him is faded and he looks less ghost now and much more man. He's wearing the same outfit as he always wears too, but that also looks more real than an apparition. It's as if the veil between worlds has thinned just enough for him to stand there, almost fully realised, in the dimly lit kitchen.

"You're not supposed to be here right now," I croak, lowering my mop.

He shrugs. "Neither are you."

"I'm just finishing up. Ensuring the place is spotless for..."

"Aww, are you cleaning up for our little date?"

"I thought it wasn't a date?" I clarify, placing the mop back in its bucket.

"Well... I don't think it would be considered a date, no."

"Then why would you say that?"

He stops leaning on the vending machine and starts slowly walking toward me. "It's pretty special though, so while not a date, it's an important night. We're going to break each other's curses!" He stops just shy of a few inches from me. His voice drops to a rough whisper. "Tomorrow night. You sure you're ready?"

"No," I admit.

"But you are going to come anyway, right?"

He doesn't wait for my answer because he knows I can't refuse him. He reaches out, seeing my glasses have fallen a little down my nose, and tries to adjust them. But his fingers pass right through me and dissipate like mist. Like a memory. I shiver all the same—it's definitely not like the silky touch I felt that very first night. This is cold. Eerie.

As I look at him, I want nothing more but to grab hold of him. Touch him back. Kiss him. This goes beyond normal attraction. My heart feels like it is pounding out of my chest as I look into his eyes.

"If this works," he starts softly, but I can sense a hint of sombre to his tone. "You'll be free."

This is true. I would no longer be aroused by rubbish. "And you'll be free, right?"

His smile falters for the first time. "I am not entirely sure. Maybe I'll get to move on to the other side? Or perhaps I will just vanish into you."

There's no time for me to respond to that. He leans in, close enough for me to feel the cool touch of his ghostly breath against my cheek. He then whispers. "Either way, I'll finally get to touch you. And that is enough."

I swallow hard. I loudly blurt, "That's not enough for me". The words come out of my mouth before I can even think about them.

He recoils with a look I can't read—something between hope and hunger and a thousand years of trash-stained tragedy. "Oh, Janitor Boy." I melt again. I am like putty, and he can have me any which way he wants. "Don't let this be anything more than us helping each other out," he whispers again, smiles, his amber eyes twinkle, and then vanishes in front of my eyes.

I spin on my heel and head to the bin. I peel it open. The kitchen is empty once more. It's just me, my mop and a cursed erection I can't explain to anyone. I adjust my jeans and look at the empty bin one more time. Tomorrow can't come fast enough.

THE GROUCH
"BIN-SPIRIT"

Chapter 8—Reservoir

It was the summer of 1979. I was seventeen, sunburnt and certain I was going to hell. At the time, I didn't mind the sound of it, if I was being honest.

Hell sounded warm, and I hated the cold. It was loud, and I hated silence. And it was much more honest than everything in the same, straight up and down, prim and proper suburban hush that was Ghoulberg. The suburb I grew up in was the kind of place where husbands all mowed their lawns with military precision and housewives would say, "Poor dear" about my mother having to raise a faggot-for-a-son like me.

She bore that burden only for a short while. I left home that year and had been living in a shitty apartment near a service station, two streets over from the supermarket and four from the school I dropped out of. Well, not dropped out...I just never went back for my final year of high school.

I worked nights hauling crates at a warehouse that smelled of raccoon piss and discarded dreams of men who failed to live up to their *dizzying* high school heights. My boss was a right prick as well. He called me *Trash*.

Most people did. Said it with a sneer, like it fit better than 'Eddy'.

I had stopped correcting him. Embraced it. I started to really enjoy the new persona and confidence it gave me.

Trash wore ripped jeans and faded yellow band t-shirts. *Trash* carried a Walkman with a copy of *'You Make Me Feel (Mighty Real)'* by Sylvester on cassette. *Trash* kissed boys in the alley behind the bins, even let them fuck him for some extra cash, but he never once called it love.

Not even with *him*.

Mark.

Mark was my first and last boyfriend. He had a job in the army and was awaiting his deployment. He smoked, wore leather-scented cologne and called me 'Eds' when we were alone, and 'Mate' when we weren't.

He said our arrangement was meaningless, and just a way to get out both of our frustrations. He said I should be grateful he didn't discard me like the trash I was.

He liked it rough. He liked me quiet and always naked, ass up, face down. He liked to see my ass when he walked in. And well, I mean, who wouldn't; it *is* a great ass. Trash worked hard to get it right for his tops. But Mark didn't care about the effort. All that mattered to him was whether I was ready for him whenever he wanted. I was never to look at him while he was inside me, or even whimper. I was his hole to breed.

Afterward, he'd shower and mutter, "You don't get clingy, or anything, OK?" and then he'd vanish into the night with wet hair and a satisfied grin on his face.

Mark was also straight. *So he said*. The only thing straight about him was his cock when it was inside me.

He left with no trace of me left on him, and he left me lying there with his scent and cum still in me. He went back home to the poor girl who he intended on marrying. I knew her as well. We would chat at the service station from time to time. Mark never knew. Like an unspoken rule, I never asked him about her. He never brought her up.

Every time he left, he said it was the last time.

And every time, he came back for more.

And me? I let him. Of *course* I did.

I was a slut. A broke, desperate, bottom-bin-of-a-boy who thought being wanted, even if like this, was better than having no one.

Mark had a fat, rigid dick. Knew how to use it too. And, I was a willing hole that needed to feel something. Anything.

Even if that thing was the expanding erection of Mark as he came inside of me. Because in that brief moment, I belonged to someone. *Meant* something to someone.

I wasn't dumb. I knew I was a joke to most men. A secret shame of theirs. A problem to be hidden and stay that way. But Mark was routine. A comfort, in the worst kind of way.

He also had a temper, and I knew this when getting into the car that sunny Thursday afternoon. It was also the hottest day on record, so I was wearing very little. A simple singlet, with the top of my chest exposed, with a thin overshirt and cutoff jean shorts.

I heard his car pull up, and the familiar twitching in my hole occurred. I was expecting to have my apartment buzzer go off when, down the street, he honked his car. Like he owned me.

And let's face it. He did.

I looked out the window, and there he was. Leaning his back on his car, aviators covered eyes. His chest glistened in the sun and dripped with sweat from the heat. Even from my window, I could see his tight muscles and his bulge begging to be let free from his shorts.

The window to the driver's seat was down. He snaked his arm in and honked again, and I got the message loud and clear. I forgot to lock the door as I rushed out of my apartment, but I didn't care. This was one of the rare occasions where Mark was treating me like a person and not his personal sperm bank.

Though if I were a sperm bank, my retention rate would be very low. Especially after Mark was finished with me. Yes, that was a gaping-hole joke. You may laugh.

As I reached him on the street, he flicked his aviators down the bridge of his nose and inspected what I was wearing. He smirked and then winked, only to put his aviators back on.

Why was he being so kind today?

He cocked his head, and I climbed into his Jeep.

No seatbelt. And *never* any small talk.

After an hour of driving, we arrived at the reservoir on the edge of town. I had heard stories from the guys I let do me for a twenty behind my work. It was a local beat for all the down-low 'straight' men to take their secret shame bottoms. It's a bit of a dangerous area with jagged rocks and snakes, so Mark gave me his worker boots. Steel capped. It was gross and made me feel warmer, but better than being hurt. It made my heart flicker even just for a moment that he cared enough to bring me a pair. He had put on his own set as well.

We get out the car and made our way to the reservoir. Here, gay men could be free to fuck to their heart's content, hang out with like-minded men, and if their bottoms were lucky, they'd *get* lucky. Your top's friend would top you while you topped their bottom. Gay slut math. Keep up. Or, if you were *extremely* fortunate, they'd swap positions and go at it all over again with you.

Mark was possessive, and I wasn't that lucky. He barely tolerated the idea of another man looking at me, let alone being inside me. And he especially hated if I looked at other men.

"Don't you get any ideas, mate." He said as he got closer to the indiscernible chatter of men ahead. "You are mine. I own you. If you be polite to my friends, I will fuck your brains out later." He leaned closer, and his hot breath blew into my ear, making my hole quiver. "Misbehave, and you won't be able to walk!"

"So, either way, I'm taking your big, meaty one?" I reached over and squeezed his cock through his shorts. I shouldn't have. He didn't like it and gripped my forearm, pinching it like a warning signal. I winced.

He let go and smiled, taking off his aviators and hooking them on his shirt. "Come, follow me."

We veered from the main path and walked on a side path down to the water, near a gazebo. It was beautiful. Stunning even. I couldn't wait to go swimming naked. Everyone here swam naked and fucked in and out of the water. I looked around and, by the reservoir's edge, in the trees and bushes, groups of men were already getting it on.

We wandered back, and Mark saw some people he recognised. We walked over, and he introduced me to his friends. They were all men in their late forties. And yes, they had amazing bodies for their age. Like their entire purpose in life was to work out and look good.

And a lot of them wore the tightest clothes imaginable. I couldn't help but stare; full hogs on display, and I was a hungry hole for some porking. Mark noticed, and when his friends walked off and spoke to others, he grabbed me from behind, dragged me to the gazebo and wrapped his bicep around my throat, to untrained eye it would look like an affectionate hug, but I was basically in a chokehold.

"What did I say?" he whispered into my ear.

"Are... you... *testing* me?" I struggled to ask back. I shouldn't have. He gripped my neck in a tight burst then released. I gasped for air. I knew he liked it rough. So did his friends, who noticed us and came back over.

"Your bitch getting out of hand there, Mark?" asked one, causing another to turn around.

"I have to slap mine sometimes," said another. "Remind him who's in charge!"

It was one thing having Mark use me as his cum receptacle. It was another hearing these men talk about me like I wasn't even there. Like I wasn't even a person. Just an object. It was a quick yet devastatingly crushing epiphany. I wanted out, and I made to leave, but Mark grabbed my hand.

He grabbed my hand. He never grabs me like this.

Not in the rough way like he normally would. It was gentler. Apologetic. I was taken aback, and after placating his friends, he urged me to leave with him.

He took me to a secluded part near the reservoir, a clearing just before the forest started, away from the crowd. He let go of my hand and then walked forward.

"I am sorry for bringing you here. I just wanted one last moment with you before I..." he stammered but didn't look my way.

"Before you what?"

"My deployment is starting early. I have to leave tomorrow." He spoke.

I nodded but didn't look at him.

"You're gonna be OK though, right?" He asked in the voice he used when he was trying to be kind. It was the same one he used when he begged me back inside when I ended things the first time. "Eds?" He approached me, and I looked up at him.

This was my moment to actually do something with my life and be rid of this man, who had just been using me day in and day out for nothing but to satisfy his needs.

"Dunno," I said. "Don't think you would even come to my funeral if I died tomorrow if I am being honest."

He snorted. "Not even if it was on garbage day, *Trash*."

He stepped forward, oddly tender for him.

"But you know it's not because I don't like you. Just in the world I'm from, they don't understand people like you and me. I have learnt to blend in."

Hide who he was, he meant.

A question bubbled up inside me. I needed an answer to it . If he was going off to join the army, I wondered how his betrothed was feeling?

"How's Judy taking the news?" I asked and regretted it instantly. I broke my one unspoken rule that was never meant to be broken. He didn't know I knew who his fiancé was, let alone her name. And now the truth was out.

"How do you know about..." his eyes flickered from concern for my wellbeing to pure rage. He continued, but with venom in his voice. "Not that it matters, but she *is* coming with me. We are both starting a life in the town I'll be deployed to."

I laughed. I shouldn't have. He never liked it when I laughed at him.

"What's so funny?" he asked.

I couldn't control it anymore. All the years of being used and abused. Laughed and spat at, discarded. I had enough. I didn't care anymore.

"The fact that you are running away with your fake fiancée, when you are nothing but a closeted fag who loves to use weaker guys as your personal cumdumps." I couldn't stop myself. It was word vomit. "Come out already, Mark, maybe you'll finally be happy for once in your life." I make to turn, and I am pulled backwards and spun back around. My heart fluttered. He was choosing me. Then it sunk in a crushing defeat.

The first hit was an open-handed slap. It was a warning, but I couldn't register it. Mark was strong, and he liked it rough. He didn't know his own strength, which made him dangerous. I knew this in getting with him but never thought he would actually be this level of dangerous.

Violent.

I was seeing stars. Dazed, I stumbled back and fell over into the dirt. I don't know how long I lay there. But it didn't matter.

The second hit was a rage kick to my stomach. The steel cap made the blow hurt so much more. Then another and another round of more. I tasted blood as I tried to fold in half and protect myself.

I don't even remember the last hit. I just know it was enough to have the lights turn out.

When I woke up, I was in a bin.

Not metaphorically. It was a literal dumpster behind the service station. I lived nearby. I must have been thrown in - my body had crumbled between milk crates and split rubbish bags. There was rotting, soaked cardboard on top of me.

I don't know how long I lay there. Maybe hours. Potentially days. I remembered seeing the sky change colour a few times between the gaps in the cardboard. I tried to call out. Tried to scream. He must have also stepped on my throat, because nothing came out but a muffled, unintelligible cry.

So, I lay there. Probably bleeding internally, aching beyond belief. Praying that if this was how I was to die, someone would at least find me and pull me out before my body rotted away.

Then I slipped away.

Deep into the abyss as my brain and other organs finally gave up. As did my soul. *They* had won. *They* had defeated me.

Trash was taken out. Mark finally got what he wanted out of me and left me there in the bin, discarded.

Dying was also the weirdest experience I have had.

There was no bright light. No voice from above. No montage of childhood memories. Just stillness as my lungs collapsed from the weight of the rubbish. As the final breath escaped my lips, all I could remember was... I wish I had loved myself more. Found my mother and forgave her. Then... I rotted away. I became *one* with the rot and trash. I guess trash is what I deserved to become.

Chapter 9—Reborn

When I awoke again, I wasn't me anymore. There was no pulse. I did not need to breathe. And my body was transparent. I held a hand up and could see the trash underneath it.

Somehow, I was still here but now sitting upright in the same bin. My knees to my chest, surrounded by trash that whispered in my ears.

All the discards of life spoke to me, and their voices were loud. A banana peel told me about its missing innards. A receipt sobbed about being torn in half. And a cigarette butt begged me to suck on it with my sweet lips.

The bin itself? My last resting spot?

It was a casket that cradled my spirit—and all these other spirits—in the living world.

Humans would pass by and offload more trash into the dumpster. I recognised them, but they could not see me or even hear me.

At first, I thought I had gone mad. Maybe I had. The first time the rubbish truck came, I was picked up and collected. But a few hours after, I would fall asleep and would wake back up in the bin. I was trapped here. And it felt like forever.

Over time, days, weeks, months I managed to hold on to things within the bin and not allow them to be emptied with the rest of the trash. More discarded souls joined us along the way and told me all about how wondrous it was living in the afterlife.

"You weren't discarded!" a Q-tip said. It was covered in earwax and some red liquid...probably blood. "You were merely transformed. This was a metamorphosis! A spiritual transition."

"What am I? A ghostly butterfly?" I looked at it and was reminded of the newly added message on Q-tip packaging about not inserting them into the ear canal. Had this one been used and gone too far into someone's ear?

Another voice spoke, and I turned. "No, he's a Grouch! A Bin-Spirit!" A mouldy ham baguette inside of a takeaway coffee cup said.

"I'm not grouchy!"

An empty vodka bottle clanged against the side of the bin. Its voice sounded cartoonish and goofy. "Not 'grouchy', a *Grouch*...Gawsh, they don't make spirits like they used to! This one ain't listening a darn bit."

I misheard. "What's that?"

"A spirit who lingers where they died." The vodka bottle said smugly. "But the death has to be linked to a particularly violent action. Otherwise, you'd just be a lost soul. A drifter, sad and aimless. Like a sock missing its pair, chewed up by the dryer."

"Charming." I muttered and grabbed the soggy newspaper beside me and threw it at the bottle. My brain didn't register at the time, but over eight years had passed.

"You died in a bin," added a cracked makeup compact, its shattered mirror reflecting fragments of my new form.

I hadn't seen my reflection since I was alive, and if I weren't already dead, the sight would have made my heart stop. I was completely translucent, and everything from my hair to my skin gave off a greenish hue. My eyes had black rings around them, truly channelling my inner Fester Addams, and I looked entirely drained of all life.

Which *duh*? I was dead. But it still shocked me.

"How you died made you perfect grouch material. Reborn from rejection. Baptised in the garbage. Congratulations!"

Something inside me shattered.

"I don't want to be a Grouch or a Bin-Spirit." I groaned, trying to stand up in the pile of garbage bags, only to feel the weight of... nothing. No bones. No muscles to pull me along. But there was still resistance. Like I was glued to the bottom of the bin.

"I was just at the reservoir where Mark..." My eyes went wide, and my voice halted as I heard his name leave my mouth. "I wasn't meant to die!"

"It really doesn't matter what you want," sneered the compact.

"What matters is what The *Rot* wants."

A long silence stretched across the dumpster. I didn't understand this place. And my brain could only take me back to my final few days of living. I could no longer remember much before that, just feelings. As if it were slowly decaying away like my body was.

I was at the reservoir, and Mark took my hand in a way that I could remember was kind. Gentle. I turned as he pulled me back, and I was happy...I *remember* feeling happiness.

I didn't understand why I had been brought to this place. This new world wasn't just filth and fragments; it was discarded memory.

Everything in this bin contained a story.

Including me.

I could still smell the heavy exhaust fumes from Mark's Jeep. Hear his laugh through clenched teeth. Then, it flashed before my eyes.

The taste of copper in my mouth.

I held my fingers to my lips and then to my side. There was an ache in my ribs. But it was worse than my mortal injury.

It was shame. And it curled around me like a blanket I couldn't unwrap from my body.

I should have fought back or screamed for help. Should have valued myself more and not ended up with someone like Mark. Should have never got in his Jeep that day. Scratch that, I should never have let him near me or let him fuck me so good I craved him.

I should never have let him cum in me.

But I knew that what we had, him being my boyfriend, wasn't real. He used me.

Mark, hell, *no one* cared about me when I was a human. I was trash.

And the irony was, I was now a spirit that inhabited trash.

But I refused to allow myself to wallow in my grief over my death. My newfound friends Vodka Bottle, Q-Tip and Compact pulled me from my stupor and taught me all they knew of this rotted world.

Over the following days, I learnt the rules of The Rot or, as I liked to call it, *The Rotted Hellscape known as the Afterlife.*

Grouches weren't just ghostly leftovers. We were echoes sharpened into weapons. The more shame, pain and betrayal we carried into our deaths, the stronger our form was. And I was *powerful.* Incredible, even.

The next time the bin was emptied, my afterlife world expanded. I learnt from Vodka Bottle about The Rot network—something I could travel through. I could move from bin to bin.

My first few jumps were wobbly, but soon I met other Bin-Spirits and traumatised souls. I was shown the extent of my abilities and learnt almost everything there was about being a Grouch.

We weren't simply vestiges of brutal deaths–we get created when something within us refuses to decompose. That something is a hunger deep inside our soul.

Hungry for what? Vengeance.

Even though I no longer had a heart, I had an unfulfilled purpose. Soon, I became more confident in my abilities that I could wander the streets and leave the bins for short periods. These periods grew as I learnt I could hitch rides with litter along the street that would get caught up in the wind gusts.

I haunted backstreets and sewers.

I travelled aimlessly, long and wide, and watched the city move on as though I had never existed.

They all forgot about me.

That young boy named Eddy.

He died. He became what everyone called him.

Trash.

Trash now lived in the bins and spoke with rubbish. He made friends with crumpled paper, or used condoms thrown out with semen still in them.

His mother never found his body. Never looked for him.

And Mark?

Never found guilty of his murder, and got to move on entirely.

On one rainy night during my travels of the city, I caught a ride on an empty soda can rolling down a long hill. It and I landed on a small suburban street, and the can had made its way into a small garden with overgrown weeds.

As if fate had its way with me like everything else has had in my existence, this wasn't any ordinary person's home. I escaped the can and glided to the window, where I peered inside.

It was Mark. This was his home. But, Mark was much, much older than when I last saw him. Greying hair and wrinkled skin.

Time and the years out in the sun had weathered him. I pressed my hand against the glass. I wanted to get a better look at him.

Time stops mattering when you're a spirit, so I hadn't realised how much time had passed since I died. I would wager it had been twenty years by now. But I knew one thing. He didn't deserve another day of happiness.

His contented look twisted something inside of me. It wasn't just anger, but something deeper and more primal. Rage. And it just got worse as I was drawn back to the can, which started rolling away again, pulling me from his home.

I was reborn at that very moment. A new purpose.

I was going to haunt him.

Claw my way through inside his house, and I'd make him see me.

Then make him regret the day he ever murdered me.

Chapter 10-Revenge

Now that I knew Mark was happily living nearby, near the very bin he dumped my body in, revenge was all I could think about. They say you shouldn't seek revenge because it consumes you. But those people probably were never murdered by their boyfriend for the crime of mentioning their wife-to-be's name and standing up for yourself.

Most people would have moved on after twenty years. But I'm not most people; hell, I'm not even a *person*. My soul definitely had not moved on, and given what I know about being a Grouch and being the manifestation of vengeance, I won't rest until Mark is lying dead in a pool of his own blood.

Every time I closed my eyes, I saw him alive, smug, married. Happy. I thought of him married to Judy, fucking her, how miserable he would have been all those years pretending to be straight. With every sad thrust, did the memory of what he did to me fade from the corners of his conscience like old gum under his shoe? Or did it just make it easier to shove to the back of his mind, so long as he had a hole to fill?

Despite feeling this, I was stuck. I didn't know exactly where he lived–damn trash-magnet I am. Before I could make a note of his house, the street he was on, the trash I was anchored to blew to another neighbourhood. I couldn't do a damn thing. At least I made it back to my bin behind the service station.

Just as I lost all hope, one night, *he* came. Not Mark, but someone else who knew *exactly* how to help.

Shuffling in like some human moving a dented wheelie bin, this new spirit fell into my dumpster like he had always belonged there. When he saw me, he froze.

He had a nose ring made from a pull-tab and eyes that pierced through me. His hands looked gnarled, and through his awkward smile, I saw how black and rotting his teeth were.

"Ah I see this place is already occupied," he grunted. He held out his hand.

I didn't shake it.

He sniffed the air, and then a smile appeared on his face.

"I know you! You are the new Grouch. The one who was left here to rot!"

I stared at him. This Grouch was... something.

He had a tangle of patchy grey hair on his head that resembled furry mould, old takeout boxes for shoulder pads, rags for clothes, and his hunched features made him look ancient. He exuded an aura that reeked of piss-covered cardboard and stale resentment.

"I'm Eddy," I drawled. "But people used to call me—"

"Trash?" he cut in, wheezing a laugh. "Yeah, I know. You have developed quite a name for yourself down in The Rot."

"Guess my reputation precedes me?"

"Our little slice of afterlife is just one big gossip zone. Dumpsters, drains, junkyards, loading bays... You know, anywhere the discarded things go, we manifest. And boy, it has been a long time since a good Grouch manifested!"

"Well, yeah, I know how I came about." I replied instantly and nestled myself deeper into the garbage bag couch I had fashioned for myself. "I have some... *baggage*, like all Bin-Spirits."

"Yes. You harbour a deep resentment. Trust me, I was the same."

Was? My ears pricked up. "How did you process it?"

He laughed. And it was loud, bouncing off the sides of the dumpster and through me.

"Process?" he laughed again, wiping a tear from his ghostly eye. "I didn't do *shit*. I accepted my fate. And here I am, wandering The Rot." He flourished his arms in a semi-pirouette, and I just stared at him.

He looked back at me, and he folded instantly. "Fine, if you must know. I was too late for my revenge. My murderer killed himself out of guilt. He preferred to take his own life than to face the crime of raping me."

"I'm sorry."

"Don't need to apologise to me, Eddy, you didn't do it. It was my uncle. He was sick. Evil. Twisted, like most who rape children."

We sat in silence, letting the words settle within me. I had never met anyone so forthright about their death.

"I'm Grumble, by the way," he added. "I've long forgotten my human name."

I shook his hand this time, and it was nice to actually touch something, someone again.

"Is this what we do now?" I asked. "Rot together in bins until we lose our minds?"

"Most do," he replied, then tilted his head. "Unless you've still got something you want to get off your chest?"

"I do. It's Mark. I know where he lives, so now I can-"

He looked interested now and leant forward. "Ah, so you want to see the man who killed you?"

"Not just see him. Destroy him." I nodded.

"Do you know what you are?" he asked, leaning even closer again, and whispering as if people were listening outside. "You're a Grouch, yeah, but more importantly, you are *Mould-bound*. You've got a vengeance thread coiled around your soul. Until you face–Mark, was it–you're stuck as a Mould-bound Grouch forever."

"I don't just want to face him," I said. "I want to ruin him."

Grumble's grin split wide. "*Now* you're speaking my language."

Grumble was the first thing resembling a friend I'd had since dying. Crass, greasy, unfiltered. But he listened.

"I want him to pay," I told him as we sat shoulder-to-shoulder on a mound of damp cardboard under a flickering security light. "I want him to remember me every time he breathes."

"You're not the first ghost to crave a haunting," Grumble said, picking his ear with a chopstick. "But most never get the chance. All most can do as Bin-Spirits is move trash around, and that doesn't exactly make people run for the hills. They just think we're low-level poltergeists. Fucking Nullers will ruin this world. There will be no revenge if Mark doesn't know it's you, right? You need help. Lucky for you, I know a guy who can help. He does recon for the Spilled Spirits."

"Spilled Spirits?"

"They're a network of bin dwellers and drain creepers, like us. We exchange gossip and trash intel."

"...You're joking."

"Do I look like I'm joking?" he grinned, his blackened teeth making another unwelcome appearance. "We'll find your Mark. And then? We take our time."

Chapter 11—Revisited

G rumble arrived back with flair, slipping through the crack in the bin like a ribbon of shadow and popping up in the bin beside me. He was wearing a crown fashioned from a coffee cup lid and holding a damp envelope in his teeth.

"Mail for you," he chirped. "Took me a while, but I finally found a route to Mark's house that doesn't require you to litter hop. One soul-scented target gained express delivery." He spat the soggy paper onto my lap with exaggerated ceremony. "Your murderer's got curb appeal."

I wiped bin juice off the envelope and read the scribbled details. Mark's address was scrawled in psychic ink, visible only to the vengeful and the dead. It was two suburbs over.

"Chirpy doorbell too," Grumble added, peering over my shoulder. "One of those that sings when you press it instead of ringing. Like a dying bird trying to smile."

I groaned. "Of course he'd have a singing doorbell."

We rode the waste stream like sewer tourists until we popped out of a storm drain across the street from Mark's house.

I finally had the chance to see more, unlike my fleeting time with the empty soda can. Everything about this place made my ghostly skin crawl. He lived on a quiet street with a cream-brick house. The front lawn was trimmed like a dollhouse garden. The flower beds were lined with polished white stones. A wooden welcome sign dangled from the porch that read 'Home is Where the Heart is'.

I was thrown out like rotting takeaway, and here he was with hydrangeas and happy endings.

Grumble leered at the garden as if it owed him money. "Wife. Two kids. Son and daughter. A golden retriever named Muffin," he muttered, picking up and licking a cracked yoghurt container that must have made its way here during a storm. "Also, he composts."

"I fucking hate him," I say.

After this visit, the haunting began subtly.

I started by watching. In silence. In the shadows. Now that I knew where he lived, I could follow him, learn his routine. I would perch with judgement in bins outside his office, curled in discarded lunch wrappers at his gym, hiding in the pedal bins in the change rooms.

It wasn't just about fear. It was about knowing him. Knowing who he'd become after killing me. If he even remembered me?

He walked around as if nothing had happened. He was confident, clean-shaven. Faintly smug. A man who wore leather loafers without socks.

He joked with the baristas. Called his coworkers "mate."

I imagined shoving him into traffic every time he smirked. Grouches don't get intrusive thoughts. We *are* intrusive thoughts.

Grumble scaled rooftops like a demon squirrel–if he had a big bushy tail like one, it would be twitching. He'd watch him from a distance to see if I missed anything. When he came down, he told me everything he could. "He's a surface-scratcher. No depth. Everything's performative. Watch him."

We did. For days.

Mark left Post-it notes for himself like 'Buy milk!' and 'Tell Lisa I love her!'

Who was Lisa? Probably his daughter.

He sent emails with way too many exclamation points. He called his dog "Lil-Muffin-Wuffin baby girl" in a voice that made my soul curdle.

It was... infuriating. Why did he get happiness and to live, when all I got was to rot!

He wasn't broken. Not haunted. Not even guilty, just *fine*.

But his wife was never seen around the house. I don't even know who his wife is, if he even stayed with Judy or if it's this mysterious Lisa woman. His children moved out... he was alone with his dog.

So, I escalated my plans.

Mark was a creature of habit, and every day he would pick a ham sandwich to eat on a park bench.

The same bench.

Every day.

Without fail.

So, I knew I could begin haunting him even without Grumble catching on. There's one trick fellow Bin-Spirits showed me, and I've been dying to try it out on someone who deserves this. And if he does what I hope he'll do after I try this new trick, I'll be able to take my haunting to the next level.

I waited in the bin nearby and then, like clockwork; he sat down. I slithered out and touched the bread as he went to take a bite of his sandwich.

The moment it touched his tongue, it decayed. Rot bloomed beneath his saliva, spreading across the bread like revenge. He took a bite of it, munched on it slowly, and then I could tell by his sour face that something wasn't right. As he looked down at his sandwich, he saw that the bread had gone completely black and green, the meat slimy and greying.

He spat it out in a furious panic.

"Fucking gross!" he said, spitting out the food, and tossed it into the bin. The same bin I was in.

It still had some of his saliva on it. This was exactly what I'd hoped he'd do. Grumble taught me I just needed a part of him, something he discarded, to form a connection. I figured Grumble meant something sentimental, but surely some of his discarded body products would work too?

I licked up his saliva globule and, like a sudden kick to the head, memories knocked my skull and flooded my mind. They weren't mine, but they were of me.

A connection was made.

It was like I had gone back in time. Mark and I were in the throes of a pounding session. He had me on all fours, facing away from him, but his massive hands were over my eyes, around my neck, pulling me back. His tongue was deep in my throat after he had just eaten me out, my ass sweat all over my face. His heavy breathing in my ear. Hot and wet. His thick cock deep inside me. As he groaned and erupted inside me, he gripped me tight. Like he never wanted to let go.

Then the memory shifted.

He pulled out. Zipped up. Lit a cigarette. He didn't even look at me as he went to leave.

"See ya, *trash*!" He said.

I jolted back to reality, sitting in the bin next to his sandwich bench, discarded rotted food still in my hands. I drop it. I was seething.

Grumble's voice startles me—at some point during my vision, he had joined me in the bin. "Thought I lost you," he then whistled. "That was a damn good ride." He glanced at me and grinned, not his usual aloof or cheeky grin; this was sharper. Like a lightbulb had turned on in his head.

"You just memory bonded with Mark. That was much faster than any Grouch I've seen. You're *in* now!"

"Memory bonded? In now?" I asked him, and he shuffled into an open burger box like it was a couch. "What does that mean?"

"It means," he said, flicking a discarded lettuce leaf off his shoulder, "you can get inside his head. Play tricks on him. Haunt him for real."

And we did.

We hopped a ride on a rolling piece of trash and then rode the sewer line to Mark's home during the day. The plotting of his true haunting could finally begin.

Chapter 12 – Recognised

Watching a man go about his nightly unwinding routine was not the most bizarre thing I ever did. Plus, I am dead, so don't judge me. Gotta know your enemy so you can successfully haunt them, right?

Mark brushed his teeth with the same aggressive enthusiasm he used to fuck me. It was rhythmic. Unapologetic. *Rough*. His gums bled, not that he seemed to notice the pain, and finished with a rough spit out into the sink. He can probably still taste the mouldy sandwich in his mouth. *Good! I hoped it lingered.*

As the water washed away his spit, so did another way to get a mental connection to him. This man was being extra cautious in his home. Something on top of my haunting must have happened to him since we last interacted.

I was behind the mirror, inhabiting a discarded tissue he left in the built-in cupboard part of the mirror's vanity. I could see through things at will. The mortal physical realm was meaningless to me now that I had learnt how to travel across it once again.

He held up a piece of paper, and I peered through to see the intricate handwriting on the other side. It was from Lisa. She was his daughter. *I don't know why, but that made my heart flutter.* The letter gave me much more insight into his life. Judy and he had obviously separated. I could only make out that they still love him but cannot accept that he has chosen 'this lifestyle'.

Had he finally come out and accepted himself being gay? *Well, at least he did something right for once.*

I found my sea legs, so to speak, and now that he was vulnerable, this was my chance. But because I was sitting in the mirror, I could have some fun. I could alter the angle of the reflection ever so slightly. A normal person wouldn't pick up on it. But when someone looked closely, someone who was vain? Yeah, they would notice their reflection was off by a mere fraction, lagging just enough that if you stared long enough, you'd feel queasy.

If this Mark is anything like the Mark I knew, he was still full of himself. It was only a matter of time before he noticed. He hadn't yet, but soon he would.

"Are you *sure* about this?" Grumble hissed. He's also in the room, squatting on the towel rack with his bin-juice-dripping coffee-lid crown of glory tilted askew. "You really want to dive in now? This guy flosses like he's punishing his gums for existing."

He should have seen how he fucked.

"I'm not waiting anymore," I murmured.

Grumble winced as Mark rinsed and spat again. "You haven't even prepped the final phase yet. No fridge-rot. No closet whispers. No symbolic trauma breadcrumbs. You're skipping straight to psychic confrontation and spirit-dong theatrics."

I looked him dead in the eye. "He's starting to *feel* me. I can tell. I saw it in the twitch of his jaw when the mirror shifted."

"Could've been gas," Grumble muttered. "He ate beetroot salad with dinner."

I ignored him and figured it is time to move. I drifted down through the air like forgotten lint and glided toward the laundry hamper. A plan was forming in my head: as well as rotting food completely, I've been told that once I have a strong enough mental connection, I can visit his dreams. That, followed by an echo of a manifestation, then maybe—*maybe*—some light possession to force him to picture me again and hear me say something like:

You murdered me, Mark, and now I'm going to make you pay!

Too much? Dramatic? Well, I'm sure after being murdered you would be too.

"You'll regret this," Grumble warned, hopping off the towel rack onto the bathmat with a squelch. "This sort of vengeance without proper prep, it doesn't play nice. Once you're seen, you can't be un-seen."

That's the fucking point. Isn't it? Is this what I want? I shook my head. Of course, that is the point!

But before I could slip through the crack beneath the door to reposition, Muffin padded into the room.

She froze. Her neck fur rose. Ears flattened. She saw me.

Really saw me.

Golden. Fluffy. A betrayal in dog form.

Grumble bolted behind the laundry hamper.

"Oh, fuck no," he whisper-screeched. "It's a Golden-Retriever. They're like medium-grade exorcists with a waggy tail. I've seen one banish a Spectre just by looking sad."

I always wondered if pets saw things humans never could—this confirmed it. If I were alive, I'd have been pumped.

Muffin growled. I stood my ground.

She charged. Not at me, *through* me. Her incorruptible good-girl energy hit like divine bleach. My form flickered. I stumbled, destabilised, momentarily pure.

"Nope!" Grumble squeaked. "Nope nope nope!"

He dove for the shower curtain and climbed. "You're on your own, Trash Prince. Tell your vengeance arc, I loved it. I did. But I'm not getting exorcised by a fucking Labrador." He picked up the pace and then swung like a gymnast on the rail. He leaped with pure precision through the open window and then...

He vanished.

It was just me. Muffin. And Mark.

"Muffin!" Mark growled, and it made my heart leap from my chest. "What's gotten into you, girl? Come on." He grabbed her by the collar and took her to her bed in the laundry room.

Mark climbed into bed, turned out the light, and settled onto his back.

I had followed him and hovered in the shadows near the ceiling. My limbs trembled.

This was it.

My one moment to enter his dreams.

To haunt him.

Chapter 13 — Replayed

I knew from the past when Mark had inadvertently slept over; he dreamed little. Well, I assume he didn't; he was a sound sleeper. Must have been one of those people who had a clear conscience and could fall asleep instantly. But that night, I made sure he would dream of me. He didn't have a choice.

Mark tossed in his sheets as if guilt was tucked in beside him. His bed creaked with every movement. The room was hot, and sweat clung to his collarbone like regret, glistening in the moonlight peering through the gap between his blackout curtains.

There were so many crumbled tissues and dirty laundry in Mark's room that my corporeal form manifested stronger than ever. I was still a spirit, but I could leave his wastebasket entirely. I hovered, *lingered* just above the ceiling fan, coiled like a storm cloud in a haunted painting.

I watched and waited. Let that moment ripen.

He tried to fight it; he squeezed his already-shut eyes tighter and threw his blanket off of him. His shirt was lifted, revealing his stomach. He had got chunkier over the years, and his furry stomach was frustratingly hot. I wanted to reach out and touch him, but I controlled myself. He was muttering to himself, but that only egged me on. I slunk down like a snake seeking its prey, and then I stopped.

Mark was always ruled by his body. And right now? It was betraying him. Despite being fast asleep, his hand slipped under the waistband of his sweatpants. He reached further and took hold of his cock. He let out a sigh and, in his reverie, shifted his pants down and pulled out his massive cock. *I missed that thing so much.*

He began stroking himself. It made my incorporeal spine arch like it used to for him. He let out a small grunt and then whispered a word. "Eddy."

He said my name!

Then, in the moonlight, I spotted it.

A bead.

A silvery shimmer.

Slick, glistening. His cock twitched, and out oozed a pulse of pre-cum welling at the tip.

Bingo! This was my entry point. I had done it with his saliva. His cum would only be more potent.

I dove.

My spectral form slinked towards Mark's bed. I landed on his legs. A familiar position I have been in before. I wanted nothing more than to reach out and grip that cock again. Run my hands along his shaft and take it in my mouth. Lick the tip and swallow it. But I shook my head. I was on a mission for revenge, not to have ghost sex with Mark.

I slithered forward until I was face to face with his cock. He was furiously stroking, and the pre-cum was building and covering his glistening head. I stuck out a finger and touched the warm smear of silvery liquid.

Wasted bodily fluids were just as good as discarded items, dirty laundry or even trash, and it bound me to him. His filthy sex dream was my invitation into his mind, and I swirled my finger around the tip of his cock, causing him to groan louder and arch his hips upwards. With a mere touch of my finger into his pre-cum, the world around me went stark black and his dream world opened around me.

We were back at the motel we both visited.

It was cheap. Tawdry. Nostalgic in a way that made me sick. Wallpaper was sweating off the walls. A lamp flickered.

I stood in a corner.

Silent.

He hadn't placed me yet.

Not this spectral version of me, anyway. But the dream echo version of me? Absolutely.

There I was. My past self was already on the bed. Face down, ass up. Waiting. Just how Mark ordered.

Mark didn't question it. He just undressed. Shirt off. Belt undone. He let out that little grunt he always made when his cock got fully hard, like he was proud of it. Like it was a weapon of ass destruction; a sword to slay his enemies.

He climbed onto the bed and grabbed the echo-me like he always did, like I was just a toy for his pleasure. A thing.

That was how I knew the actual Mark hadn't changed. So, I took the place of my echo. Dream logic met my spectral-trash-powers, and his mind couldn't resist me whilst I still gripped onto the head of his dick in the real world. I became the body beneath him.

I needed to take control of this situation, and I knew just how to surprise him. My body twisted around, and I grabbed his wrists. I flipped the dream-us and rolled him onto his back, and the Mark outside of the dream caused the dream him to also react by gasping.

"Eds?" He wheezed like the wind was taken out of him. I'm not quite sure how I managed to flip him and still keep his erect cock inside of my hole, but somehow, it stayed put. In fact, Mark got even harder.

I know it was a dream, but it was so tempting to keep this going. To ride him until his hot cum shot through me. My legs straddled his thighs, and I could feel his thundering heartbeat throb through his cock and flex my hole open further.

"What are you doing?" He asked, his breath laboured.

"Getting what I came for." I grinned wide, and his eyes lit up.

There was no harm in indulging him a little, right?

It's been so long since I felt any form of connection. I would be denying myself this if I finished too soon. It was just like old times, at least the better part. He and I were connected on a lustful level.

He thrust his hips up, and I felt every inch of his dick slide through me. I let out a groan, and it only made him hornier and more powerful. He held my hips in place as he continued.

I grinned down at him as he thrust. "You want this hole, don't you?"

He nodded his head, and his cock was pressing against my ghost form like it was begging to be forgiven. Like each thrust was a reminder of the man he used to be before.

My eyes flashed open, and I pressed my palm to his chest to lean forward to his ears. His hands were gripping my waist, grabbing my ass and pulling me in closer. I whispered slowly.

"You left me to rot. So now you'll rot in me!"

His eyes went wide, but he couldn't stop thrusting into me. *He was getting off over this!*

He gave one last almighty thrust, and then he moaned. Loud. Ragged. I could hear his outside voice coming through. A name caught in his throat like a globule of mucus that couldn't be coughed up.

And then he came.

Violent.

Convulsing and ruined.

I had claimed him. Made him, this moment, *mine.*

The surrounding dream shifted, and it was shattered around me. Mark was waking. I let it happen and shifted back into reality.

Chapter 19—Resurfaced

When I phased out of Mark's body, he was in a daze. I glided to the corner of the room, hiding behind his dresser, and watched him. He was lying there, his chest covered in his cum, confused about what had just happened. His arms were at his sides as his chest quickly rose and heavily sank.

"What the fuck!" He said, looking down at himself, finally realising the mess he's in. A thick serum of cum was embedded in the fur of his chest and stomach.

He rolled over to his bedside table, grabbed a handful of tissues, and dabbed himself clean.

When I stood up, I had accidentally knocked over an empty beer can from the top of his dresser, and he looked up, mid-wipe.

"Who's there?!" He blinked. It was still a bit of a habit for me to freeze when eyes flew my way, but when I went and moved away from the dresser, he did something nobody's ever done before. His gaze followed me.

He could *see* me.

The air grew icy, just enough to cause goosebumps to form on his forearms. I looked down at my hands and then held them up and twisted them. I still had that greenish glow, but my form was flickering, but then, for what I can only assume was out of my desire for him to see me, I became more solid. Still a little translucent, but I was otherwise corporeal.

He didn't scream, nor did he flinch; instead, he widened his eyes. There was an ache in his voice.

"Eddy?"

I shifted forward; my feet hovered over his carpet. My form was clean this time. No rot or grim or green glow. Just me. The way I might've looked as if I was allowed to live.

He sat up, shifting back slowly, and threw his tissue to the side and quickly readjusted himself. He covered his body with the blanket. Stayed still, cautious that any other movement would scare me off.

"Hello Mark." My voice echoed slightly. That was new. Must be the new form, because I swear, I'm not doing this voice on purpose to make Mark's haunting even scarier. Although it was definitely a bonus.

"What are you doing here?" He asked, voice cracking. "I looked everywhere for you. You haven't aged a day!"

Looked everywhere for me? You fucking liar. I had felt a lump form in the pit of my gut that travelled up through my mouth and steeped as an insult. I wanted to hurt him. Make him feel as much pain as I did when he had thrown me in the bin. I eyed him up and down. "Whereas you have let yourself go."

That must have caught him off guard, because he snorted, "Ha!" Seeing that I didn't laugh with him, he composed himself and shook his head.

"When I left you there in the clearing after I slapped you, I felt awful and came looking for you, I swear. I came back to look for you, but the other guys said you left."

Was he *gaslighting* me? "Don't bullshit me, Mark. I know what happened. You beat the living shit out of me and left me to die in a bin!"

Mark stammered. "W...*what*?"

"Are you deaf, fucker? You *beat* me. *Killed* me. You never kept your anger in check!"

He hung his head and shifted in the bed. I hovered forward, coming into contact with the edge of his bed frame. I was drawn to him. Is this shame, regret, confusion he's feeling? Did he truly think I was alive this whole time? Why would he be confused about something he clearly did?

After a long pause, he finally looked up at me. Looked at how I was floating, finally seeing me for the spectre I am. "You think I killed you?" He swallowed. "I didn't, I swear."

I froze. For a moment, I believed him. For *one* moment.

"Bullshit! I'm DEAD, Mark! And you did this to me!" I screamed at him with enough volume, grit and rage that showed how much pain and anguish I was in. Muffin barked from the laundry, but Mark didn't tell her off.

He shook his head, looking down. "I hit you, yes." He looked at me, his eyes full of honesty. "Only once. I regretted it. Was angry. I hated myself for it. For a lot of things. But I never meant to—"

"So, you *did* hit me?" I spat. "I didn't just imagine it!"

"Yes. I was ashamed. I treated you like trash—" he winced at the word, making him pause for a moment. "But after I slapped you, I left. When you fell... I ran away from you to my car and drove off. I didn't kill you. I think something happened after I left the clearing. I didn't know you were *murdered* there, Eddy." Tears were welling in his eyes. "You have to believe me."

It made no sense. Rage and grief had written him into my memory like a villain. But it wasn't my blood on his hands. Now I wasn't so sure. And it wasn't just written on my face.

My form flickered like static.

"What do you mean you didn't know?"

"I saw the missing posters your mum and her friends put up. I was even brought in for questioning, but they cleared me of any charges. I thought... I hoped...." He pressed his fists into his forehead. "I thought you ran away like you always said you would. I thought my moving away had inspired you. Then I found out you had died. They found your remains in the dump."

"I was left in a bin to rot" I whispered. "This entire time I thought you did it. How can I believe you? What if you're lying now?"

He stared at me, unshifting his gaze. My eyes locked on him. And then he did something I wasn't prepared for.

He held out his hand, palm up. Not to touch me, but in offering.

"Look," he said. "How can I prove it wasn't me?"

I stared at his hand as if it was a curse in itself. A trap. A test.

But something in me trembled. Some old instinct from when I believed he could be better. That maybe he hadn't been the one. That maybe, all this time, I'd been rotting with the wrong man's sin etched into my soul.

I stepped forward.

My fingers hovered above his palm.

I hesitated.

He didn't move. He didn't blink. Just waited.

And I...

I took hold of his hand.

Our fingers touched, and the world changed around us once more.

His awake mind was messy. Strange. Like a junk drawer brimming with loose change, postcards, broken pens, old love.

I floated through it, half-formed, tethered only by his touch. His regret. Mark was beside me, his mind cracked open willingly, offering no resistance this time. "I need you to see," he whispered.

The room fell away. His bed, walls and house were gone in a blink. It was replaced with a haze of static and fog. It was thick. We moved through it, and at some point, it felt less like we were moving forward ourselves and more like we were gently being pulled. Memories flew by us.

His mind wasn't orderly. Some memories were of him as a kid, some of him at his current age. No surprises there.

It wasn't a reel of chronological flashbacks or a curated archive. It was a dumpster fire of suppressed emotion. Locked with chains, doors and taped-over regrets.

We stopped moving. I peered ahead of us, and the memory, hidden deep in the back, called to us. This is what Mark wanted me to see.

I shot forward and realise I'm at the reservoir clearing. The sun was bleeding through the treetops. Everything looked golden.

Soft. Too soft.

Like his memory was trying to romanticise the last time he supposedly saw me. Or was he hiding the true nature of it, the way I saw it, from himself? Grief and guilt had a way of distorting memory, after all.

I stood to the side, spectral and still.

Mark was driving, parking up the car with me in the passenger seat. We had arrived just as I remembered.

Then the current Mark standing next to me noticed too. And he flinched.

"This was our last good day before..."

"Good day?" I asked. "This was the worst day, the last time I thought I was safe."

The memory flickered. The sun snapped, and we were suddenly standing under a shade-covered gazebo. He was ordering me not to get any ideas with his friends, not to speak unless spoken to. My eyes saw past-Mark grip my arm, the warning. It made past-me wince.

"See?" I snarled. "This is the man I remember. The aggressor."

Mark hung his head in shame. "What was I thinking? I just wanted everything to be right. Wanted you to be *mine*."

"You were a coward. Too worried about what others thought, even around others like you. These men were all sick, violent. Abusive. These were not friends. They were cruel sadists." I stood in front of him and made him look at himself. "That included you."

"No! I...I..." he stammered. He was shaking, and I didn't let go. "I had a bad temper back then...I..."

Everything went hazy. Mark's mind was taking us elsewhere. A graveyard.

Past-memory-Mark walked through the graveyard and, like it was tethered to him, my body followed him.

He stopped at a small grave plaque in the ground, and I shuffled around him to look at it. Nothing prepared me for reading my own grave plaque.

It was smaller than I thought it would be. Simple. Tilted a little to the left, like even in death no one gave a fuck about me. The inscription read:

EDWARD "EDDY" JAMES
Loved by few. Forgotten by too many.

Even if that were true, that stung.

Memory-Mark knelt in the dirt as if it owed him answers. His fingers were filthy; nails packed with soil. He wasn't crying, not really. But his whole body looked like it had been weeping for years.

"I'm sorry," he whispered. "I should've been stronger. And been with you for real. Protected you. I shouldn't have taken you there."

I stepped closer. Reflex, maybe. Habit. I still wanted to comfort him. Even now. Even after everything. He bowed his head and breathed out my name like a prayer.

The haze returned, and the surrounding scenes changed as if Mark's grief was unpacking before my very eyes.

When the surrounding haze dissipated, I knew exactly where we had ended up. It was my mother's front room. You never forget the smell of your childhood home.

My mum sat in her old chair, the one with the floral cushions and the busted spring. She looked older, frailer, but her eyes still had that spark. That steel.

Mark was kneeling beside her, holding her hand like it was the only thing anchoring him to the earth.

"I let them take him," memory-Mark said to my mother, shame spewing from his throat. "I stood by. I didn't swing. I didn't scream. I didn't stay. I just let him be a victim to those sick assholes!"

She said nothing at first. Just looked at him with that quiet knowing she always had. I wanted nothing more than to reach out to her and say I am sorry. Tell her I love her. Tell her in my last moments I thought of her.

"I didn't know my son by the end. I regret that most of all. I regret not having given him a safe space to live in. A home to be himself. Love. I regret not having loved him like he deserved." My heart, if I still had one, wanted to burst out of my chest. "He was thrown in the trash, and died alone, did you know? But my son wasn't trash. He was my son!" She was crying now, and Mark tightly gripped her hand.

The real Mark stood next to me and took hold of my hand. "She loved you."

I murmured some sounds in agreement. A pained cry.

Another scene bled through, this time the motel. It was our first time.

The same cheap sheets. The same fucked-up dynamic. I saw myself in the mirror, hickeys down my neck, bite marks across my shoulder. But the worst part?

I looked *grateful.* I wanted to hurl up my stomach contents, but I had not eaten in years.

I grabbed him. The real one. Here. Now. Beside me and made him face me.

"You let me believe that what we did was love," I whispered. "You knew I had nowhere else to go. And you made me feel *wanted*. But only on your terms. Only when no one else could see us together."

Mark's voice shook. "I know."

"I wasn't just trash, Mark."

He looked at me. Eyes full of something finally breaking open.

"I *know*."

I turned away from him. Let the motel fade. The clearing dim. Let the weight of what *could have been* collapse like a building behind us.

Then there was silence. I let it extend around us until it echoed in our ears. The kind of silence where you could hear your heart thump through your chest. The silence where you can hear your blood pumping up from your feet and back down again.

I paused. I knew what I needed to do.

For him.

For me.

To move on and overcome my past. I needed to say the words. And mean them.

"I forgive you."

It echoed around us and hugged him.

He gasped. A real, ragged sound.

"But not because you deserve it. But because we both need it."

He nodded. Trembling.

I stepped closer. My voice is quiet now. Bitter. Human.

"You should have been *kinder* to me. Not just at the end. From the start. You shouldn't have treated me like something to hide. Something to use. Something you could just throw away."

"I know," he said again, softer.

"Because I was never trash."

His eyes met mine. And he said it, not with excuses, not with deflection. "I see that now."

"It's too late for me, but you are still alive, Mark. You need to go live your life and stop living in regret and in the past. I am fine. I have accepted my fate."

The memoryscape trembled. Cracked at the seams. Light bled in from the real world.

I looked down at our still-touching hands.

One last surge passed between us. And I knew he felt it too. Not peace. Not healing.

But truth. Truth about my death. Truth that he and I were never meant to be together. Truth that I was going to be OK. That I am OK.

And that is exactly what I had needed to move on.

OSCAR & EDDY

Chapter 15 — Bin A Long Time Coming

I didn't move for what had felt like hours. He and I sat on the floor of my janitor's closet. I had come in on the weekend, as we had devised. No one else is here but me, him, and the howling wind and rain outside. It is a perfect backdrop for what had been a very emotional story.

I take a deep breath as if I had held the air in my lungs the entire time. I rub my eyes; they were dry from not blinking.

Eddy had just...told me everything.

Not just in words, but in a sort of psychic data dump with full surround sound. Tragic lightning. Overdramatic musical score. And bonus trauma projections.

He showed me who he once had been when he was alive. What he became. And what he had to do to get here.

I am half-wrapped in my janitor's overalls; the arms are tied at the waist. Covering my chest is just a thin singlet. It is quite warm in the janitor's office, even for a dreary day.

He stands up across from me now. Tall, hot, and glowing in the dark in a low-budget afterlife kind of way. He truly is from the seventies. He is still the same bin-dwelling spirit to me, still moving like one. But something about him had shifted.

The weight on his shoulders had gone. The quiet around his eyes is now full of noise.

He looks like he has finally let it all go. And I knew from my own burdens that telling someone is the first step in forgiving yourself.

"I am glad you got to speak to him," I murmur.

Eddy tilts his head. "About what?"

"All of it. The slap. The murder. The forgiveness. It was very much the trash prince redemption arc you obviously needed."

Eddy pauses, then grins at me. "I didn't even think it would work. I went into it wanting to make his life a living hell. But he wasn't the villain after all. Don't get me wrong, he was an asshole, and if I could do it all again, I would never have let him fuck me. But hindsight is a beautiful thing."

"So does this mean you're free?" My voice dips, a little too hopeful.

Eddy glances around the room. "Almost." He looks contemplative. Like he is plotting something.

I let it hang in the air. It is thick with everything we had not yet said. It's the silence you only get after a storm, or a séance, or a cosmic therapy session conducted via bodily fluids.

After some time, I break the silence.

"Something that has me wondering..."

"Yes?"

"What happened to... Grumble, was it?"

Eddy smiles and hangs his head down. It is an actual smile, one I can be in front of forever.

"He is now the King of the Rot."

"...you're making that up!"

"Nope!" he looks proud of himself. "He earned it too. After Mark's dog Muffin spotted him, he ran and accidentally fell through into the sewer kingdom, and he defeated the reigning Toad Emperor in a game of Trash Chess.

"That *also* sounds made up."

"He sent me the postcard. Invited me to be his right-hand man."

I raise an eyebrow. "A postcard from the King of the Rot?"

"It was mushy, banana-scented."

We both snort and, just like that, whatever tension left between us breaks.

He comes to sit beside me. Not touching, just close enough that I can feel the heat from his form.

And for the first time since I've met him—since he haunted my bin, since he showed me the worst of himself—he looked *ready*.

Not to scare. Not to seduce. Not to possess.

Just to leave.

Eddy says nothing at first. Just stares at the closed janitor's door like it holds the answer to something neither of us were ready to ask.

Then he turns to me, a flicker of concern threading through his expression.

"There's still your curse."

I wrinkle my nose. "Right. Yes. The whole reason we're here. I was kind of enjoying the not-talking-about-it part of this evening."

He ignores me.

"It's tethered to a moment," he says. "A memory. A core imprint of shame, or pleasure, or both, that's where most bin curses bind. To break it... you need to go back. Deep. Find it. Unlock it."

I blink. "You want me to... memory dive?"

He nods.

"And how exactly am I supposed to do that? Visualise my trauma while licking a pizza box?"

Eddy looks at me sideways. "No. That's more of a Monday thing."

"...Then how?"

He hesitates.

I squint and realise what he wants to do. "No. No. Whatever it is, I already hate it."

Eddy runs a hand through his ghoulishly green curls. I notice that it's not actually green–he's a dark brunette–but his ghostly glow makes it look so. "To form a link strong enough to open the anchor memory, I need a tether."

"Define tether."

"A bodily fluid."

"Oh, gods."

"It worked with Mark—"

"Don't you *dare* say—"

"—and I could *technically* enter your mind through your—"

"Nope!" I jump up so fast my back cracks. "You are *not* dream-walking through my cum, thank you very much!"

Eddy, unbothered, grins. "We could just kiss?"

I pause. "...That also sounds like a trap."

"It's not."

"Feels like one."

"You're cursed," he points out.

I sigh. "Fine. But if this ends with me drooling into a memory vortex while you rifle through my brain pantry, I'm revoking your closet privileges."

He tilts his head. "You have a brain pantry?"

"Metaphorically."

Eddy steps closer, his gaze warm now. Gentle. Steady.

"It won't hurt," he says. "But you have to let me in."

I swallow.

The room feels too quiet again.

His hand brushes mine, ghost-light and careful.

And I realise... I wanted to let him in.

Even if it means facing whatever memory I had buried so deep it turned me into a walking garbage hard-on. Even if it means trusting a Bin-Spirit who makes friends with used Q-tips and empty vodka bottles. Kissing him with my curse still clinging to my core may be my only hope of breaking it.

Because somewhere along the line today, I had stopped seeing him as a spirit and had seen him as someone I can love. Someone I had fallen for.

Eddy's lips touch mine like a match to kindling. It isn't gentle, but it isn't forceful either; it is *inevitable*. As if the moment had been circling us all this time, and we had finally stepped into it.

The taste is strange. Not bad. Just... old. Like smoke and rust and the warmth of summer rain on hot concrete.

His hand cups my jaw. Our tongues meet and massage each other. I am so lost in his kiss that it takes me a second to realise the lights in the room are flickering.

And then the floor drops out under me.

We're now standing in a different version of me. Not *with* me, *but inside* me. Inside my memories.

We are in my old flat, my one-bedroom that smells like mould and burnt rice. Where every surface is a monument to my lowest point.

I recognise the exact night.

My ex had just left, stormed out for good. He had said I'm pathetic. Said I'm warped. Said I got off on the *wrong things*.

He had not been entirely wrong.

I'm—my memory-version of me - is kneeling beside the laundry basket. Still breathing hard. Face flushed, body trembled.

'My' hand is wrapped around *his* jockstrap, which is sweat-soaked, threadbare, stanching of his musk. I had pulled from the hamper like some guilty treasure. Memory-me is pressing it to his face, breathing in what is left of my-our-ex. Memory-me is wearing it like a mask.

My pants are down. My shame is louder than the moans. As I stroke myself faster, huffing in Marcus' scent.

Eddy says nothing beside me. Just watches.

Then the door rips open, slamming as it swings and hits the wall.

Marcus stands there, his aura flaring like static, hair dishevelled from a night out. His eyes blaze as he sees memory-me. I pull the makeshift jockstrap-mask off one eye and stare at him.

"You sick fuck!"

I flinch. Not past-me, *me*. Here. Watching it.

"I told you," he snarls, fists shaking. "You can't *keep doing this!* I thought you wanted *connection,* Oscar—not just *objects!*"

Memory-me mumbles something useless, broken. About not wanting to be kink-shamed.

That's when he curses me.

He didn't need a circle. Didn't need a spell book. An Etsy witch was much more skilled than any you'd read in a book or watch on a TV show.

Just *rage.* He points his finger at my heart, and it's as if time had stopped. The room goes dark... the lights subtly flickering.

"Let your lust rot with what you crave most. May trash be your forever hunger."

The jockstrap in memory-me's hands glows with an eerie shimmer, then it disappears into a million particles of green light. The specks fly up and then enter my body.

Memory-me gasps, then collapses.

The curse hits like fire, honey, and filth. They tangle into one.

Everything blurs.

I moan—and remember I had liked it and I cum all over my stomach, the jockstrap still on my face. I realised in that moment I had been cursed not just by magic, but by my belief that I had deserved it.

My memory shifts yet again. Eddy tightly grips my arm, his face already paling. In front of us is my old share house. At this point in my life, I had been kicked out of everywhere I lived because of my sick desires. The room is bare, aside from a mattress on milk crates. Fast-food wrappers crunch underfoot with every step. The air reeks of weed, sweat, and something worse. Desperation.

There are... objects. Things I hid under the bed. Plastic wrappers. Grease-stained boxes. Half-melted takeaway containers I had fashioned into makeshift rubbish flesh-jacks I had used on myself. God, I had forgotten. I've *buried* all of this. Since I had been cursed, I had found new ways to pleasure myself. Then, I couldn't resist the call for attention that most trash gave me.

Eddy turns slowly. His face changes with every object he sees. The lube bottle beside the McMuffin wrapper. A condom that had been filled with bin juice, that may have once been frozen for something I won't repeat. The filthy sock I'd named "Henry", yes after my HR Manager. Don't shame me.

I want to scream. Run from my embarrassment.

"I didn't mean..." I croak.

Eddy stares at me. His eyes look lifeless. Vacant.

And then something *snapped*.

Not in the memory.

In *him*.

His memory-figment body recoils as if he'd been hit. His outline shimmers, corrupted. The soft aura he carries with him—the spirit shimmer that makes him, *Eddy*—crackles with static and turns jagged. Splintered bin-light shoots through the room.

"No, no, no, no—" I desperately try to hold him.

But he's already falling apart.

We tumble back into the real world with a crash.

Eddy staggers backward, clutching his head and shouting.

His eyes are wide, black with gold rings around his irises. They shimmer with rot.

"Eddy?" I say slowly, not sure what was happening.

He doesn't answer. His back arches. His form stretches, then convulses. Eddy's skin peels like sodden, mouldy wallpaper. His fingers elongate into clawed slivers. His clothes tear down the seams, but what emerges isn't naked.

It's grotesque.

Sludge-clung ribs. Mismatched teeth like bottle caps. A glistening crown of coffee lids and drain hair. A shield shaped like a wheelie bin forms around his torso, with holes for his legs to push out of.

"Eddy!"

He hisses—*hisses*—spitting bin juice out his mouth, then bolts away from me. He scuttles across the ceiling with a lurching, centipede-like grace, then crashes through the door. A spray of wood shatters across the ground. I chase after him. A window shattered, and the sound came from the fire escape stairs. I followed and could hear the rain and thunder still battling for dominance. Joining them was my one chance to break my curse. My shoes crunch the glass shards as I step through. The door didn't budge. My only option was climbing up and out through the window.

Chapter 16 — Vanish Binto you

E ddy's massive figure had just crashed through the window, and I followed, leaping out and landing with a wet thud, avoiding the jagged glass sticking up. As I check my shoes for glass shards, I feel my heart race. I snap around and listen out, trying to hear him through the pouring rain and clapping thunder.

I was now in a part of the alley I hadn't seen before, further back and next to the building, behind Graves & Pennington. Remnants of the previous business are here, and I instantly realise what this building used to be. It was from Eddy's story. The new owners built over it but kept the petrol station bowsers as a sort of memento, now all rusted. All this time, I've been at Eddy's bin. Where he died. He had been haunting this place longer than I had been alive. It all makes sense how he had found me.

The dark bitumen reflected the moonlight and streetlights, broken by puddles that shimmered with each flash of lightning. There's a rustling in the back corner, and my eyes catch the motion of a claw-like leg retracting.

It's Eddy. Or the monster that he had transformed into.

I approach with caution; I don't want to startle him, not when I am so close to breaking my curse.

Slowing down even further to a silent creep like I was a burglar from the Sims, the cold, wet night air pooled around me. Nearby, I catch a whiff of the smell of the big garbage bins, my brain almost short circuiting but I shake my head and do my best to keep my focus on finding Eddy.

The Bin-Monster Eddy recoils back as he sees me. I pull out my phone and ignite the backlight, slowly shining it along the ground towards his feet. Mouldy shadows ooze from his joints. Dripping gunk pools beneath his claws. I drag the light up and see that the skin and musculature of his limbs are elongated, twisted, patchwork from a hundred different unloved, untouched things. His torso is now covered in what appears to be some sort of warped wheelie bin. Discarded objects cling to his body: banana peels, cartons of milk, newspapers from over forty-six years ago, and more. On his head, a crown made from coffee cup lids. In full view, I can now see his transformation had completed, and he hunched like a crumpled aluminium can. He had sharp fangs, and black ooze spewed out. Through his teeth, he shot a globule of ooze and then hissed.

It was a warning not to approach. But I didn't care. I see through this form. I see *him. Eddy.* The man I have fallen for in ways I cannot describe in words, but my cock did it's very best to translate them when I am around him. I am aroused emotionally and physically. Spiritually as well. He is still a ghost made of trash, after all. My perfect man.

"Eddy..." I whisper gently.

He lets out a low, wet, defensive snarl. It was painful to listen to and he backs further into the shadows, trying to shield away from me, but he knocks over a precariously placed wooden pallet that had not yet made its way into the recycling. The noise echoes through the back alley.

I then just had a thought. If this is the same building, then the original bin Eddy died in... It's now long gone. *Replaced.* It's been so long since the 70's. Which means... Eddy doesn't have a true place to call home. His death site is gone.

Even though I know the owners would not have known about Eddy, I want nothing but to find the owners and punch them. Make them hurt for stranding Eddy, leaving him feeling discarded and abandoned once again. But I know this isn't the answer.

Eddy doesn't need more violence. He needs love. Connection. Safety. He needs... me.

"I'm not afraid of you." I say to him, reaching out a hand.

He hisses once more, but it is softer this time. One clawed hand curls over his chest as if he is trying to hold himself together. 'Goo' drips from his fingertips.

I shuffle my feet closer. One step. Another.

The closer I get to him, the more I can see what's hiding behind his eyes. Behind the sludge. The gnarly fangs. The wheelie bin outer shell, harbouring his inner spirit and keeping it protected within. His broken soul begging for someone to love him.

But there, underneath it all, is Eddy. The tenderness. His cheek. His hurt. And the most important thing about him—his hope.

As I speak, my voice is shaking. I wasn't scared. But I was worried he wouldn't come out of this form, that he couldn't see me anymore. That he can't feel the connection between us. "You're not trash. You never were." He shifts like a disgruntled teen. "You were just... lost. Looking for someone to connect with. To be with. For someone to actually see you for you. To hold you safe in a world that didn't give a damn."

He trembles.

"I see you now, and all I know is, I want to be that someone for you."

The Grouch's monstrous form quivers, spasms—like it doesn't know whether to collapse or run.

I step into a puddle, but I don't care. I approach slowly, carefully. Like coaxing a wounded animal to be rescued.

"I could be that for you," I say, my voice barely above a mutter. "I could be the one who keeps you safe. Who doesn't run from you. Who doesn't dispose of you like trash."

Eddy stares at me. His eyes shift. They return to their normal amber colour.

I smile at him. He was still in there.

His body jerks once, like he just hiccuped. The storm's even subsiding–the hard rain simmering to a gentle pit-ter-patter.

And then, along with a guttural sound like a sob torn from a drainpipe, he steps forward, the wood pallet crunching under his claw feet and falls into my arms.

Black sludge smears across my singlet, some dripping onto my half-worn janitor outfit. His form is still radiating heat, rot and grief. But his hands—claws—cling to me like I am the first loving thing he's felt in years.

I hold him tighter.

"You don't scare me," I murmur. "Not even like this."

The Grouch whimpers... "Oscar."

The sludge pooling beneath Eddy's monstrous form evaporates, curling upward like steam. His jagged silhouette trembles, then softens, as if the truth of my words were re-shaping him from the inside out. I stroke his face and push his hair out of his eyes.

"You are beautiful."

"No," Eddy murmurs, voice garbled. "No...don't."

But he's already changing.

The twisted claws recede. His gnarly limbs shrink back into something human. The bin-rot stink fades into warm petrichor and ozone. And then... light blinds me as I hold him.

Bright, chartreuse, and strange. Eddy's body gleams. Translucent, fracturing into stardust at the edges.

His time was ending. With me, fleeting.

I clutch his fading hand. "Don't go. I need you."

He looks at me with tears in his eyes, but they weren't sad. He was happy. "I wasn't supposed to find peace.

"But you did."

Eddy's lip quivers. "Because of you."

I don't know what to say. So, I say nothing. I just lean forward, breathing him in, holding on to every second I have left with him.

"Thank you for seeing my truth," he breathes.

And then he kisses me.

Not with hunger, or haunt.

Not to enter my mind or stir buried memories.

Just to kiss me. Person to person. Man to Spirit.

And I kiss him back.

The shimmer brightens. He's blinding, beautiful—and then the surrounding light dims.

He's still here. Still *him*.

Just... real now. Solid. Warm. Human.

And then I understand. The curse broke.

His *and* mine.

He holds up his hands and twists them. "I am solid!" he lets out a laugh.

And I pull him closer to me, helping his stand and holding him in my arms, jumping ecstatically on the spot. "You're alive again!" We both laughed and looked like saturated fools dancing behind a bin in the rain.

Eddy pulls back and looks at me. "Oscar, there is something I have wanted to do with you since we met."

"Anything. Name it."

"Sleep with me."

My stomach flips. We're hidden, out of sight, so it's not exactly out of the question. And right now, all I want is to hold every inch of him, anyway. But... "We can go back inside and—"

"No!" His voice is urgent, and it catches me off guard. "Let's do it here." He turns and looks at the pallet on the ground and the cardboard poking out of the nearby bin.

Our eyes meet, and we both have the same idea.

Beneath the moon and now completely calm sky, with trembling hands and hearts too full to speak, we undress one another, not with urgency, but admiration. Skin against skin. One man's trash is now my treasure.

His skin no longer flickers with bin-static or clings to shadows. His eyes are wide and alive, a kaleidoscope of memory and hope. I cup his cheek. It's the first time I've touched him without slime, without grime, without the stench of death between us. And he leans into it like he's been waiting his whole afterlife for something that simple.

"I think your curse is broken," I breathe.

Eddy nod. "Yours too."

He looks down at our hands, our interlaced fingers. "Do you still want me?"

I don't answer in words. I kiss him again. Slower this time to get to know the shape of him. The taste of what had once been grief that had now been rewritten as grace.

He gasps against my mouth in what I figure is a surprise. From what I know about him, I don't think anyone has ever kissed him like that.

I guide him gently to the cardboard we laid on the pallet behind the bin; the ground is still sticky with phantom residue, but we don't care. This isn't about the setting. It's about the feeling. The trust. The way his body arches into mine, seeking contact with devotion, not desperation.

My fingers trace him like a map.

I start at his ribs. Then, the curve of his hip, then up to a small scar beneath his collarbone. He flinches when I find it.

"You, ok?" I ask, pulling back my hand.

He shakes his head. "No. It's just... no one's ever touched me like this, or asked me that, either. I feel... desired, but not just sexually. I feel like I matter."

My throat catches. "You matter," I say. "You absolutely matter."

I undress him slowly, piece by piece. No rush. No tearing. Just quiet reverence for every inch of his reclaimed skin. He watches me with eyes that sparkle, not with his Grouch magic, but with emotion. Each layer I shed isn't just clothing. It is fear. Shame. The weight of years spent believing he is trash.

And when he is finally bare beneath me, trembling in the moonlight, he looks... free.

I let him undress me too, fumbling at first, but curious. Gentle.

Like I am something precious, not just convenient.

"Can I touch you?" He asks.

I nod. "Yes."

His hand slides across my chest. Down my stomach. Not with lust, but with awe. He whispers little things as he explores me with his mouth and tongue—compliments, surprises, apologies for not suggesting this sooner.

"You smell like spring."

"It's the lemon disinfectant-"

"No, I can smell that, but there is something else underneath it all. Your scent. Inviting. Warm like a spring afternoon."

I kiss his wrist. "And I can feel your kindness. Bravery too, and hope."

His eyes well up.

We move together carefully, slowly, our bodies finding rhythm not from instinct but from listening. A fingertip. A hip roll. A breath. There are no demands. Only invitations. No performance. Only presence.

He keeps checking in, asking if this feels OK, if I need more, or less, or to stop. I do the same. And every 'yes' is sacred. It is the opposite of what he'd told me about Mark. About all of them.

This isn't transactional. Nor survival.

This is connection. Love.

Behind a dumpster, we finally make love for the first time; Eddy relinquishing his fears. I grip his legs up around my waist and guide my cock into him, slick with my spit. The moon watches over us like a soft voyeur, and I see his eyes roll backwards as he takes me. It is the most beautiful thing I've ever seen.

His breath in my ear with every thrust is just a signal of our connection growing deeper and deeper. I don't want it to end, but my arousal had got the better of me.

Eddy reaches down and strokes himself as I thrust into him harder and faster, but in that gentle way out of love, not lust.

We finish together, breathless, hands clasped. My dick slips free, slick and heavy, saturated with warmth. The warmth of him. He leans into my neck and kisses me. I feel the last remnants of the curse dissolve like mist as the sun rises.

I glance at the bin. There's no more arousal at the sight of trash, no more bin-slicked shame.

Just us. Oscar and Eddy.

Two broken things who have finally stopped feeling disposable.

"It's been a long time since I've felt this." I speak.

"Don't you mean *Bin* a long time?" Eddy laughs, and I do too for the very first time in a very long time.

We say little after that. We don't need to.

Eddy lies beside me, his head nestled against my chest, our legs a messy tangle of clothes and warmth. His breath is steady. Slower than before. Lighter.

Like it's trying to unlearn the weight of centuries of shame he had held onto.

I card my fingers through his curls, softer and a darker brunette now that they aren't made of lint and that ghostly green bin-sheen, and press my lips to the top of his head.

"Thank you," I breathe.

He hums. "Of course, Oscar." After a long moment, he speaks again. "You set me free."

I feel it too. Not just the breaking of curses. But something deeper within me. A released soul. A lifted burden. A reclaimed life. I feel like myself again. My body moves with ease, and it doesn't feel like I am dragging around this meat sack that had only responded to the scent of decay. I can see the world around me and its beauty once more. And the one beautiful thing I want to keep is Eddy, in my arms, forever.

His hand finds mine. He places his hand on my chest, where my heart thuds for him.

And then... he sighs.

A content, final little sound.

"I think I was always waiting for someone like you," he says, voice almost too soft to catch.

I want to reply. To tell him, *me too*. But my eyes are growing heavy. The night, the monstrous form, the connection, it's all been too much.

I drift.

Holding him closer.

I don't want this moment to end.

"I love you." I slur and kiss his forehead.

And I fall asleep with him in my arms. His head rested on my shoulder like it always belonged.

When I next open my eyes, the sun has fully risen and is shining through wisps of clouds. The harsh daylight exposes the alley, making the back alley from last night appear dull. Ordinary.

My memory returns to last night. I finally broke the curse and made love with Eddy. A grin forms on my face as I stretch my arms over my head, eyes still shut, and then I'm suddenly brought back to reality as I feel the chill in the air rush over my body.

I shiver. I blink and look down.

I am naked. I shuffle backwards and realise Eddy isn't next to me. I look around, and he is nowhere to be found behind the bin. I shuffle on my knees to get a better view, and there he is, floating above the ground near the giant bin.

He's no longer solid. Not fully. His clothes had returned to his body.

His form shimmers, resembling a distorted reflection on water. Flecks of him peel away, floating off before fading completely from sight.

"Eddy?" I stand up too quickly trying to grab at him, but my hands pass through. "No, no! What is going on!"

He smiles. Just once.

Why is he smiling? The curse had broken; he shouldn't still be a Bin-Spirit right now! My heart's shattering into a million pieces, and he is *smiling*!

"Oscar," he leans down and places a hand near my cheek. My eyes flood with tears. "Thank you," his voice is barely a breath. "For seeing me."

He continues to fade away. I reach out and try again to grab, but it's like holding onto sand in a hurricane. He drifts out of view and then...

He's gone.

The alley is empty except for a naked me on my knees reaching up to nothing.

I sit there for a second, just stunned. Tears fall from my cheeks onto my naked thighs. The weight of last night and my life up to this point still imprints on my heart like a phantom hug.

"Eddy," I say, longing to hear his voice again.

But a familiar beep-beep interrupts my grieving.

Fuck!

It's the Sunday garbage collection. The truck's pulling into the back-alley carpark. He hasn't noticed me yet. But I am stark naked. And I will have the police called on me for sure if I don't hurry and dress.

"Shit!" I spit, hopping my legs into my overall pants. I don't bother doing the top of the janitor overalls up. I nearly twist an ankle as I pull on my singlet and duck behind the bin, scuttling towards the side path to the front. I probably look like a hungover rat in heat, but I don't care. By the time I peeked around the corner, the truck had done its job and left for the next alleyway.

It's just me, the empty alley, and the memory of Eddy, who had been the best thing to happen to me.

Chapter 17 - Trash Was His Treasure

A week's passed since Eddy disappeared, practically evaporated into bin juice mist, and a week since my curse had been broken. I didn't get hot under the collar staring at coffee stains on desks, or hard from the grease on a pizza box anymore.

I am free.

Yet, there is an emptiness inside me. The first thing I notice is the silence.

After I had nearly been caught by the rubbish truck, I went back inside the building. I didn't forget to clean Claudia's turmeric coffee stain on the carpeting near the reception desk. It didn't last long. Everything kept reminding me of Eddy. I couldn't stand being at work anymore. I had left and walked home to my apartment.

My mind used to ignite with arousal when I would come home to my filthy apartment. But the discarded trash I had accumulated during the time I had been cursed no longer tempted me.

It had been a strange quiet. The kind of quiet that wrapped around your chest like a corset and didn't let you have a full breath.

I want nothing more than to turn back the clock to the day we met. Warn myself not to take up his offer and spend more time getting to know him. That cheeky, beautiful man in the bin.

Had I just dreamt it all? Had he even existed?

I had settled in. Over the next few nights, I cracked open the window in the lounge room, in case some lost ghost wanted to sneak in and take up home in my house. Haunt me back to life.

But nothing ever took up my offer. Not even a gust of wind, or a shadow. It's like the universe forgot I had existed. Without the curse, everything had become still.

The air.

The trash.

Me.

I didn't realise how much I had rearranged my life, my habits, around the blasted curse until now. There had been a trash bin by the bed containing my favourite items. A shrine of filth in the bathroom. A compost bin that wasn't used for compost—it had been used for cum-covered tissues, folded with a similar respect a monk had to preserve sacred scrolls.

I had wanted nothing more than to clean it all up, ashamed of who I once was.

Now back to being an ordinary man, I had cleaned up. Scrubbing the floors, changing the dirty sheets, folding the laundry, getting rid of the jockstraps with my teeth indents in them and taking out the copious bags of trash to the bins. It helped only until I found reminders of him.

My mind flashed back to him sitting on the bin lid with his smug grin. Smirking as I ate my noodles, and I burnt my hand with the boiling water. Him cooling it with his strange bin juice ghostly sheen. Him crawling out of the bin, with that stupid look on his face like I had been the most beautiful thing he'd ever seen.

I felt the connection; the love we had shared without him even saying it. He had stared at me as if I was the sunrise he hadn't seen in forty years. I freed him as much as he freed me.

Then, he was gone.

I hadn't gone back to work for the rest of the week. I couldn't face the office and the reminders. Instead, after I cleaned everything up, I had wandered the apartment in the last outfit I wore when he disappeared. Claudia kept blowing up my phone, asking how the weekend was, but I didn't have the energy or desire to tell her. She must have been concerned, because as the days bled by with half-assed responses on my part, her texts grew more and more frequent. At some point, I had turned off my phone.

For some days, I had laid on the couch and let the hours rot away, in hope I would too. I had woken up on the floor often. On some days, I had eaten dinner on the toilet. I watched the ceiling until my eyes burned. Nothing on my streaming services was good enough to distract me.

I had gotten lost in my thoughts about losing someone who wasn't even meant to exist. Someone who had died decades before I had been born and yet made me feel more seen that any living person ever had. Someone who had been called "trash" but was absolutely a treasure.

I tried to jerk off to the memory of us when we finally had sex. Just to feel something. But my dick was like a taffy pole and wouldn't cooperate.

Turns out my arousal, now no longer cursed, is dampened. I broke one curse but find myself with another.

Heartbreak.

I had longed. For *him*. And only wanted to be with him. My hands, porn, *nothing* did the trick.

Tonight, I hit a new low. It's Friday. I open the fridge, and at the sight of rotting vegetables I had forgotten to use; I am reminded of him and burst into tears.

Then, just as I shut the fridge, there's a knock at my door. I panic. For a second, I hope that somehow beyond reason he is there. I let my heart feel something foolish, because I deserve this... happiness.

I deserve happiness. Don't I?

But my heart sinks as I open the door.

It's Claudia. I'm surprised and happy to see her, of course, but disappointed for a split moment that she's not Eddy.

She had brought me food—jam donuts, and a thermos which I think has soup—and a pack of tarot cards in a raccoon-shaped velvet pouch.

Her hair is braided with ribbon and feathers, and her eyes look at me with a kind of kindness that isn't pity, its concern, and something even closer to love. She's dressed exactly how I imagined her outside of work: a sleek, elegant silhouette in flowing black, like a modern-day Morticia Addams, if Morticia shopped at occult thrift stores and moonlit markets.

A sheer lace shawl drapes over her shoulders, catching the light like spider silk, and a silver pendant glints at her throat. She's all velvet and mystery, the kind of woman who smells faintly of ash and freshly burnt sage and always knows the right thing to say.

"Thank fuck you're not dead. I would have had to eat all this by myself."

Scratch that; maybe she doesn't. I groan internally.

"Uh... thanks," I reply as she steps inside like she lives here. We don't hug. We don't need to. She just hands me a jam scroll and then sits cross-legged on my floor across from my couch like my house is her personal coven and she is the *Supreme.* I sit on the floor across from her and smile as I take a bite of the donut.

I want to cry. It's so delicious, beyond anything I can imagine. How long had I been without a proper bite to eat?

"So... what happened, Oscar?" She asks me, and my heart wrenches in two. I tell her everything.

"I miss him." Finding myself admitting this after I finish explaining, my voice cracks somewhere in the middle, and I'm already holding back tears. "He was utterly, tragically... beautiful... and thoughtful in ways I didn't even realise I needed."

"You were in love with the Bin-Spirit." She says, nodding as if that is the most normal thing in the world to happen. Which maybe for our world now, it is. I don't know what's normal and not now. Hell, all sorts of supernatural creatures are out in the open now, so why *couldn't* I be in love with a ghost?

"I...I still am."

Claudia takes out a candle that smells like rosemary and burnt sugar. She lights it. "Love like that doesn't rot away, Oscar. It burrows its roots into you, deep. You grew from it, and that's why your curse broke."

She looks at me, and I can feel a tear streaking down my face. "I don't know who I am now."

She reaches out and takes my hand. "You're the same man I met a year ago, who at least now won't get hard over a coffee cup," she says, and I let out a chuckle. "You're different now, though. Better. You're softer, cleaner. You let someone in behind the walls you put up. Oscar, you let someone see you in all your trash and glory. You saw them back, and it changed you. Both of you."

I don't want to cry again. But the tears fall anyway. And they come hard and ugly—I cry in that way when someone who is close to you is suddenly ripped from your life. I cry like you do when you see a heartbreaking moment on a TV show, the kind that changes the show forever. *I* had been changed. Forever.

Soon, I run out of tears and all I'm doing is sobbing, but I'm so exhausted from everything. They're leaking out of me like sap from a tree—slow, and quiet. Claudia passes me a tissue.

I blow my nose hard. We have our own little vigil for Eddy. The Bin-Spirit who changed me. The Grouch, who had been anything but grouchy. He had been full of life. Full of joy. Full of love.

And I? An uncursed man, but a man who wakes up crying.

That is enough for now.

Chapter 18 – Bin Alone

C laudia had not stayed long, but she didn't need to. She had asked for a key, and I obliged and found her my spare. The weekend had come and gone, but by Monday morning, despite still not wanting to get out of bed and face the world, I needed to get up for work. At least I find the courage to say the words I've struggled to accept aloud.

"Eddy is gone."

I clutch the pillow in my bed to my chest. It is the only pillow I had not washed yet. It smells damp, like he once did. Mixed with dust and my sweat. *Or are those tears?* I lift my head and inspect at the stain.

I replay that moment repeatedly in my mind. I bargain with myself, begging nobody in particular for him to return. To change what had led up to that moment. But he had spirited away faster than I could process. He faded away, dissolving in the morning sunlight.

I bury my nose deeper into the pillow and breathe it in as if, if I smell it hard enough, it will somehow bring him back to life.

It doesn't.

It only brings me a headache, and heartache.

Life doesn't pause for the heartbroken, especially over the already dead who manifest as a spirit and haunt the bins in the office. And so, like all things, I have to return to my old reality.

I go back to work.

Here, no one says anything to me. Nobody speaks to me unless they need something cleaned.

Claudia gives me a long look but doesn't push. The accountant on level 4 had put in a cleaning request to get the stains out of the kitchen grout. I do the job without a fuss. I empty bins, clean stains, refresh toiletries. The motions are muscle memory at this point.

Easy.

Automatic.

As my hands work, my head is somewhere else. Somewhere darker. Quieter.

The trash is quiet too. I hate that I no longer hear Eddy's playfulness throughout the day. There is no low giggle from the recycling chute, no annoyed sigh from the mop bucket, no greasy fingers trying to tug at my belt while I am elbow-deep in someone else's mess. I had gotten so used to his presence, his little hauntings, his crude flirting, that now without them, the world feels... grey.

Not black. Black would've been better. Dramatic. Cathartic. But what I'm dealing with is grief. Wet cardboard sorrow. Everything is dull and soggy and too quiet, like a streaming service asking if *I am still watching*. Obviously not.

When my shift had finally finished, I came back to my apartment and tried everything to snap out of it. I watch my favourite YouTube videos: trashy food reviews, cryptid conspiracy theories and old reruns of that weird 90s dating show where everyone dresses like vampires. I don't even laugh. Just stare hollow, wondering if *he* is watching these videos somewhere too.

For a few days, this goes on. As Friday rolls around, I realise I need to do something else to distract myself. I text Claudia, and she hatches a plan.

I go out for drinks with two staff. I let them drag me to this small queer dive bar where the music is too loud; the patrons vary between supernatural and not, and the air reeks of smoke, sweat and cologne. I even let a hot guy flirt with me. He has broad shoulders and a filthy laugh and keeps touching my arm with intention. I smile. I flirt back. I really try to feel something.

But I can't stop comparing the lines on his face to Eddy's smooth, youthful face. I am not paying attention to what he says, but just how he is behaving. He blinks too slowly. The smell of his cologne makes my nose curl. None of it is right. None of it is *him*, but I let it happen, hoping that going through the motions will help me move on.

As Claudia had reminded me before we arrived, "Sometimes you have to get dicked down by someone else, to no longer have life dicking you down instead."

I kiss him in a stall. Just to feel something. *Anything*.

He sucks me off. I struggle to cum, but it's an empty feeling.

The silence presses in around me, us, as I zip up my jeans. A hollowness echoes inside me. Cumming into that guy's mouth had meant nothing. I had no connection to him.

He isn't Eddy.

I had rushed out of the stall before he could ask me my number.

The next morning, I wake up and immediately trip over my phone charger cord. My phone flings across the room, and I almost stumble over. I quickly dip and grab my phone, then go into the kitchen. There's a crusted mug on the counter I don't remember using and three takeout containers that might be sentient by the looks of them. I throw them in the trash and turn around, leaning against the counter. The apartment smells faintly of disinfectant and loneliness.

I shuffle through it anyway. Each step sounds too loud, like the place is trying to remind me it's empty. The bin in the corner is just... a bin; no sexy ghost men will ever come out to free me from my grief. My whole apartment feels like a stage set for a life that had already ended—every object perfectly placed, every surface too clean.

It isn't my home anymore. Just a place I come to sleep off my days.

I had thought going back to work would be the answer, but I am still hollow. He'd been everywhere; now he is nowhere.

I cleaned the whole place again. Not because I want to, but because I think maybe clearing out the last remnants will help. A sort of spiritual exorcism through disinfectant.

It doesn't help.

It just makes the silence louder.

On Sunday, I impulsively called Claudia hoping for some guidance. I hang up before she answers. I can't handle human company, even though I need it.

She arrives anyway without being invited.

She doesn't knock. She just lets herself in with that key I had lent her last week. I hear her shuffle behind me–she's found me on the couch, wearing the same hoodie I hadn't taken off in days.

She looks at me, says nothing, then hands me another homemade pastry and sits down beside me.

"Is this grief?" I ask her eventually, mouth full of almond croissant.

She shrugs. "Looks like it."

"He wasn't real, though."

She raises an eyebrow. "Wasn't he?"

"I mean, he *was*. But not... you know. *Real* real. Like, he was a ghost."

"He was real to you."

I say nothing and just stare at the half-empty bin beside the couch. I wish it would rattle. Whisper. Smirk.

I say softly, "He mattered. Made me laugh. Made me feel... wanted."

Claudia reaches over and squeezes my hand. "Then he was real. Curse or no curse. Bin-bound Spirit or not."

I don't cry. Not then. I had already used up my tears that morning on the floor of the shower, after I had cleaned everything but before I had called Claudia. But something shifts inside me, like a pressure valve has released. Like maybe I don't have to keep pretending I am fine.

She stays for hours. Made a pot of tea. Lit candles. And she forced a reading of my tarot, even though I hated that shit. Do you blame me? It's a result of having an Etsy witch as an ex.

Every card she had pulled had fire in it. Passion. Change. *The Tower* had come up, of course. And *Death*. And *The Lovers* reversed.

"He's not coming back," I say as she pulls a face.

"No, the Bin-Spirit isn't," Claudia says glumly. "But you're still here."

Later, just before she leaves, she kisses my forehead and whispers, "Call me when you're ready to let him go. I'll help you do it right."

I nod.

I'm not ready. Not yet.

Chapter 19—Bins of a Tether

Another week passes, but at least by the end of this week, I finally feel ready to ask Claudia to help me let him go. I had approached her desk at work, but her suggestion takes me by surprise.

"A séance!?" I shout far too loudly in the front office foyer.

The room turns to look at me. I lock eyes with a few people, but it's raining and most are returning from the office from their lunch breaks–soon, they continue their way, shaking the rain from their umbrellas or heading toward the kitchen for a cup of coffee or tea to keep them warm.

Claudia doesn't even blink.

"A séance, yes," she repeats calmly and casually, like she had suggested after-work drinks, or a cheeky tarot pull, not a psychic-led ceremony with the undead. "Or something like one. Bin-based, obviously."

Right. *Obviously*. She rummages around her desk, clearly avoiding my eyes as I stare at her with betrayal.

"I thought you meant, like... journaling. Or breathwork," I mutter, shifting my mop bucket behind me like it could shield me from spiritual responsibility. I really need to stop using it to hide myself–it's never worked out well for me.

"*Please*. Breathworks' for people whose curses don't involve orgasmic trash."

I blink. "You've said that out loud before, haven't you?"

"More than once."

She finally looks at me, expression softening. "You don't *have* to do it. But if you're still hoping for closure, this might be the way to... lift the bin lid, so to speak."

I don't answer. Don't nod. I just stand there in the foyer, feeling the weight of another week without bin whispers, or amber eyes, or ghostly limbs curling in the recycling bin.

Eventually, she hands me a paper bag. Inside is a bundle of wax-sealed herbs, a candle that is shaped like a traffic cone, and a piece of cloth that smells like burnt cinnamon and mildew.

"Tonight," she says, voice low. "Be mentally prepared."

The rest of the day passes in a fog.

I mopped a hallway I had already mopped. I had stared at a bin for ten minutes before realizing it isn't full—it is just me who is empty. Someone in IT asked if I am OK, and I responded by refilling the hand sanitizers in their break rooms and backing out like I had been caught crying in a supply closet.

"You alright, Oscar?" asks Jeff from Audit, as we cross paths by the elevators.

"Yeah. Just tired."

"You look... dimmer, somehow."

I want to say, "Fuck off, Jeff!" but I say, without thinking, "Ha, yeah, you'd be dim too if your bin-spirit boyfriend evaporated right before your eyes."

"Wait, sorry?" He pulls back and looks at me with a raised eyebrow.

"Oh, nothing," I brush him off.

He shrugs and offers me half a donut, which I had pocketed and then promptly forgotten about. It is that kind of day.

When the building had emptied and it was time to go, I stood for a moment by the janitor's closet—our old haunt. The bin is still there. But now it is just a bin.

It doesn't purr. Don't moan. Doesn't ask to be held.

I left the office without speaking to anyone else.

Claudia meets me outside the building and comes home with me that night. I agreed to her idea as I need closure. I'm keeping the metaphorical bin lid open just in case Eddy comes back, but I feel he won't and I need to find a way to move on.

Along with the original stuff Claudia showed me earlier today, she reveals some candles shaped like little frogs, salt she says is from some coastal witch commune, and a Ouija board made from an old pizza box.

"Recycled mysticism," she says with a wink, lighting the candles and placing them in a wonky circle around the living room rug. "Bin-Spirits love a DIY project."

I don't ask if this is real.

I don't need real.

I need *possible*. I need to do something about the ache in my chest that still hasn't faded. Maybe it never will.

Claudia has me sit cross-legged in the centre of the candle circle. She mutters something under her breath—half Latin, half gibberish—and pours the salt in a sloppy ring around me.

"I call on the trash that lingers. I summon the soul that haunts the drainpipes and dumpsters," she says, eyes closed, arms raised dramatically. "Come forth, Grouch of the Bin. Your janitor misses you."

Nothing.

Not even a *flicker* of candlelight.

I want to laugh. But I don't.

Claudia opens one eye, checks her surroundings, then opens the other.

"Oh, fuck!" She looks defeated. "I spoke with my mum, and she said this was a surefire way to get the spirit to come out."

"Maybe he is really gone..."

She shoves the pizza box toward me and plops an upside-down empty glass on top.

"Let's see if he still can communicate."

I sigh. "This is ridiculous."

She shrugs. "So was dating a cursed Bin-Spirit. Try."

We sit together, our fingers barely grazing the mug, and ask questions.

"Eddy, are you here?" I tentatively ask.

Nothing.

"Do you have a message for Oscar?" Claudia continues.

Silence.

"Are you... still tethered to this realm?" I ask.

The mug jerks to the left.

I gasp. Claudia narrowed her eyes. "That wasn't me."

It slides again. Just a nudge. A twitch. Then, nothing. We wait.

Eventually, Claudia leans back, removing her hand.

"Well," she says. "That's... not nothing."

I stare at the board. At the unmoving mug. "What does that mean?"

She looks at me, the bravado gone from her voice. "It means he might still be here. Or something of his. Tethered, maybe. Or just... not ready to pass."

I swallow hard. "Could he come back?"

"I don't know," she says softly. "Magic isn't a recycling policy."

"But it's hope?"

She looks at me long. Slow. Then, nods. "Yeah. It's hope."

That is all I need.

"Don't get any funny ideas, Oscar. Spirits need to be respected."

"I know," I say as I help her pack up. My intention is to have her leave my apartment immediately. I fake a yawn. "Jeez, look at the time, I am tired!" I stretch. "I should get to bed."

"Oh, of course." She stands up. "Just remember, if it's meant to be, he will come back."

I nod, say goodbye, and close the door.

My heart wants to break through my chest. That mug had moved. It fucking moved... he is here. I know it. I peer out my window and see Claudia's car missing. This is my chance.

I take out my phone and can see it is only 10:30 pm. I have plenty of time to walk back to the office and check out the back alley.

Chapter 20-Bin Lid Lifted

The alley behind the Graves & Pennington stinks of sour milk, wet cardboard, and iron. It had taken me no time to walk here, but I can tell it is late from how high the moon is. I brought nothing with me. No candle. No sage or trash to burn. Just the memory of a ghost of a man who used to rise from this very place and make me feel like more than a janitor with a curse.

It is quiet. There are no whispers, no shadows. No amber eyes peeking from the dark.

Just me and the soft sound of wind rifling through some nearby plastic bags caught in a chain-link fence like forgotten flags of a bin-bound nation.

I crouch near the bin where we had shared our first time together—if you could call it that. Where skin had met skin and laughter had met moans, where the sacred and the disgusting had transformed into something beautiful.

I trace my thumb over a faint scorch mark on the concrete. It looks fresh. I figure that is roughly where he had vanished. Or maybe it is just oil.

It doesn't matter.

I sit.

The smell of the place settles around me like a memory-worn blanket.

It's familiar. Ugly. Mine.

There are things I want to say.

Apologies.

Admissions.

Promises.

I had whispered them before—in dreams, in half-drunk monologues to Claudia, in the middle of mop-rinses when the ache had hit hardest.

But now... it doesn't feel like I need to say them again.

Maybe Eddy had never meant to stay. Maybe he had just been a spark, not a flame.

A glitch in the system? Or maybe a miracle disguised as a Bin-Spirit, with attitude and amber eyes.

Maybe his purpose wasn't to linger—but to teach.

That I'm not trash either.

That someone could want me. Not because of some cruel curse or rubbish kink. But underneath all the mess and mildew and mop water, I am still worthy.

That I am still something golden, even with rust around the edges.

I sit with that. The thought roots. I let it soften me in ways even grief hadn't managed.

The wind picks up, tossing a few stray takeaway wrappers down the alley like brittle leaves. Somewhere behind the office, a loose shutter bangs rhythmically, like a heartbeat too slow to save.

I don't move. Don't flinch. Just listen. The quiet presses against my ribs like the weight of something ending.

Then, I stand.

The bin looms beside me—old, rust-flaked, paint peeling like shed skin. This is it. The place they had discarded him–a different bin, but the location all the same. This had been the place he rose from, reborn from bitterness and longing.

And the place we had first truly seen each other.

I run my fingers over the side. The paint comes off on my hand like dust.

I want to scrape some into a jar, keep it like a memento. But I don't.

It feels wrong to disturb what might be the closest thing to a grave he'd ever have.

Instead, I place my hand on the lid.

Wait.

Lift it.

Empty.

Not just of trash. Of him.

"Eddy?" I whisper.

Silence.

"Guess you really did move on," I murmur.

I close my eyes. Let myself see him again—smirking, shirtless, filthy, bold. Green tinged hair. Mouth full of bad ideas and good intentions. Beautiful in a way that had nothing to do with logic and everything to do with survival.

How is it that a man already dead had made me feel more alive than anyone in my entire living life?

How is it that love could crawl out of a bin and still be the purest thing I'd ever known?

I don't cry. Not this time.

The ache in my chest is still there, but it doesn't consume me. My heart feels stretched, like it's making room for both grief and gratitude.

"Eddy," I say to the night, "if you can hear me—I just wanted to say... thank you."

I don't know what to thank him for specifically. For breaking my curse?

For the chaos of the last few weeks?

The love I never thought I'd be brave enough to feel again.

I stay a moment longer, letting the silence become part of me.

Then, I turn, zip up my hoodie and walk. I walk because running home at this hour would look strange. The walk home is quiet. Still wet from the midday storm, the streets shimmer under lamplight like spilled oil.

I pass various late-night animal shifters going for a walk, a group of vampire bodybuilders flexing in a gym with enchanted mirrors that show their reflections, a were-bear bakery open all night and always busy with an array of supernatural customers. The state of the current world's normalcy, a world that would be unbothered by Bin-Spirits or janitors haunted by trashy romance.

At the corner near my apartment, I slow.

Two young men are sharing fries under a bus shelter. They are the first humans I've seen on this entire walk. One leans on the other's shoulder. Their laughter is muffled by the plastic shield, but it still reaches me. It sounds easy. Joyful. Familiar in a way that hurts—but also heals.

I keep walking. It starts to spitting–not enough to make me want to run, but enough that it splashes on my glasses now and then, forcing me to clean it on the hem of my shirt.

Further up, a woman dances alone under the drizzle, earbuds in, lost to whatever rhythm that rules her world. Her coat flares out with each spin. Her joy isn't performative. It is private. I smile. It is like the world is healing with me.

A jogger passes, nodding at me.

A couple kisses in a doorway.

Life is... continuing.

And somehow, I'm not angry about it.

Maybe, I think I can have that again. Maybe not the Bin-Spirit part—though I'd never trade that chapter for anything—but the closeness.

The spark.

The ridiculous joy.

Maybe I can let myself be loved with no need to be broken first.

Maybe that is Eddy's actual gift to me.

I reach my building and pause at the front step. Behind me, down the block, I think I hear something. A faint clatter. The soft creak of a bin lid being lifted.

I turn, breath catching. Nothing.

Just wind. City sounds. A feeling in my chest like something old had let go.

I smile. Because maybe, just maybe, he is here too.

Epilogue
~ 6 Months later ~

I had never returned to that back alley. Unless I had to dump something in that bin for my job, I stayed away.

Some stories ended behind a dumpster. Now I know some relationships do too.

One day when I had emptied the bins, I found something that I kept. It was a scrap of him. Half of Eddy's coffee-lid crown from when he had become the monstrous Grouch form. In my grief, I thought everything about him disintegrated that day, but I had tucked it into my bottom drawer.

I don't know why I had kept it. Maybe because it reminded me I had felt something once. Something deep for another person. Someone worth remembering.

In the months following Eddy's disappearance, I had tried dating again. But no man had ever made me feel the way I felt with Eddy. And given the number of dates I had been on, I thought no man ever could.

But I had stopped chasing ghosts. With the curse lifted, I can finally live a happier existence. And I mean *live*.

Full breaths, deep sleep. Trips to my bin that no longer make me hard at the smell of thrown vegetables. This is freedom.

I had gone through waves of giddiness and terror.

Claudia helped fix the parts of my life I had thought were unfixable. Because who else but a medium *Binfluencer* can solve the rest of my problems? Only she, my incense-huffing, latte-scrying, psychic miracle of a friend, could. She had expunged all my records, cleared my fines and made workplace complaints of me getting freaky with trash vanish.

I still don't know how she did it.

She claimed she had stern words with the universe on my behalf. She also told me I was 'cosmically overdue' for a break.

I had asked her what I owed her. She grinned and shook her head. All she had to say was: "You can't afford me. So, consider your debts wiped and never involve me in your sordid affairs again. Unless you know a balding, chunky bear ghost?" *She had a type.*

Oh, and I had gotten a job offer within the office. I left my agency and became the Head of Cleaning Operations. It was a title they had created for me. Nothing really had changed in my day-to-day; really, it was just a fancy title for a guy with a clipboard bigger than his mop, and more money that he knew what to do with.

With the promotion, the office had stepped away from the agency entirely. That had meant that I needed to hire someone else to help. I had left the spot vacant for weeks, maybe on purpose. Maybe I didn't want to walk past someone else's trolley, someone else's bin-juice footprints. Someone who wasn't *him*.

I had rejected every applicant. HR must have got infuriated with me, because they turned to another recruitment company for help. An hour ago, HR had informed me that my new employee is starting today. He is due to arrive any minute now.

I didn't expect a lot. It's probs some young twink looking for some quick cash, or some older guy with a bad back who won't last the week.

People assume that being a cleaner is easy. They never understand the ritual of it like I do. The rhythm and intimacy of maintenance. The power of noticing what others discard.

My door clicks open. I mentally prepare myself and ensure my expectations are low.

Then *he* steps in.

My heart stops, trips over itself and falls face first into my stomach only to land on the floor.

He has wavy black curls. Same build. Same cheekbones. The same... *God*, they are the *same* amber eyes.

"Hi," he says. He smiles cheekily, like he always had done. "I am Edward James, here for the janitor role? But you can call me—"

"Eddy," I say simply, and his smile softens with memory. My throat goes dry.

"The Rot had owed me a favour," he adds with a wink. "Also helps when your best friend in the afterlife is the king. You... look happy, Oscar."

His voice. It's softer. Brighter. Not quite the gravel-slick whisper of Ghost-hood but still *him*. It's still the one who had haunted my workdays and had made them better.

"You remember."

"I remember everything," he breathes. "Even if I'm not *him* in the same way. I *was*. I am, and the version I became, with all the same memories... I chose this." He looks around the dingy janitor's office as if it were a chapel. "I came back here. For you."

My knees buckle.

I reach for him—gently. Like too fast a movement will break the spell and make him disappear again.

"You don't have to be around trash anymore," I whisper. "You don't owe anyone anything."

He leans in. "Maybe not. But I enjoy trash. Cleaning it now, anyway. And I like you." I stop resisting and shut the door behind him. With a grin, I let out an exhale and smile.

"Fuck it!" I throw my clipboard down behind me and drag him closer to me.

We kiss.

It isn't ghostly. It isn't cursed.

It was *ours*.

And that is enough.

There is something sacred about Oscar's janitor's closet at night. Maybe it is the flickering fluorescent light. Maybe it's the faint smell of bleach, eucalyptus disinfectant, or the muted yet ever-present rancid scent of old banana peel. Or maybe it is the fact I am finally here again—alive, warm-blooded, and horny as all hell—with the man who once made my ghost-heart, beat.

Oscar stands at the edge of the mop sink; his jumpsuit is unzipped down to his navel, his brown pubes and belly hair sticking out. The fluorescent lights above us buzz like they know what is coming.□

And what is coming would be us both.

"You sure no one's around?" I ask, nudging the door shut with my foot and clicking the latch.

Oscar just smirks. "Everyone goes home at five. It's nearly nine."

"What about those other two?"

"The Fanger and the Feline Accountant?"

"Yes."

He doesn't respond. Instead, he tugs the zip lower, exposing a flash of the base of his penis amongst a tuft of hair and then — **_FLAWP._**

His dick pops out in slow motion. Like it had RSVP'd for this moment weeks ago. Thick and veiny, he pulls his foreskin back just enough to reveal his throbbing fat head and a bead of pre-cum oozing out of the tip. I want nothing more than to throat-fuck it. Worship him.

"Not wearing any underwear?" I murmur, dropping to my knees like the reformed Bin-Spirit I am.

But he stops me with a hand on my chin. He lifts me back up, eyes soft.□

"No. This time, let's take our time. I want to enjoy this. I want to enjoy *you*."

I could've melted. Or cummed. Or both.

I kiss him. Slow and sure. No ghosts. No grief. Just us.

He tastes of honeyed coffee and smells of citrus soap. His tongue curls into my mouth as if it is claiming back something that always belonged to him. I slide against him, hungry and ready for him to slam me into the wall and for him to enter me. *Look, a bottom boy's old habits die hard. I still like to be fucked hard. But I want the heart of that man as well.*

He turns me around and gently shoves me against the shelves, right between the bin liners and the scented air fresheners.

"I used to jerk off to the smell of bin juice in here," he says between kisses to my neck.

"I know," I growl, bucking back against him. "Watched you from the bin, before I gained the courage to reveal myself."

He groans in my ear as if that was the hottest thing he had heard, his hot breath turning me on even more.

The mood had flipped from tender to feral in a heartbeat. His hands are on my ass, squeezing, spreading. Swirling his spit-covered finger around my hole. "Fuck, I missed this," he says, bending down and licking his lips.

"You've never done that with your finger," I tease.

He slides a finger inside me and says, "Now I have."

I moan—loudly. The air turns thick with heat and memory and the sharp, sour-sweet smell of cheap cleaning product and old lust.

Oscar bends me over, one hand on my lower back, the other guiding himself into me. I hear him spit into his hand, then hear the slick sounds of him coating his cock with it. His thick head rubs up against my hole. He twirls it around it, opening me slowly.

The stretch is glorious. Real.

I'm not a ghost. He's not cursed. And I can feel the initial pain of a cock going inside of me again. This was magnificent.

We are just two men in a closet, making up for all the time we had lost.

He enters me slow at first—like he is learning my human body. The warmth of it. The resistance. I'm learning too–everything is tight, and my asshole seems resistant. But I let myself sit with the discomfort. Feel myself relax around him. As I had gotten used to him, I tell him I am ready, and he went deeper. I gasp into the wall as he goes fully in me, the base of his dick pressing against my cheeks. His balls slapping mine. He gives himself a moment to feel it, then slowly thrusts into me. As I moan louder and louder with every stroke of him, he increases in ferocity. Faster, desperate, like he can't get enough. My ass stretches and tightens around his length as he pumps in deeper.

"Fuck, you feel—God, Eddy, you feel *alive*."

"I *am* alive," I gasp. "You brought me back. You trash-loving necromantic wonder."

The pace gets brutal. Glorious. Our bodies slap together in a rhythm that could summon spirits. My sweaty ass cheeks smack against his waist.

The smell is intoxicating.

Shelves rattle. A mop falls. The scent of pine cleaner mingles with musk and sex and longing.

"Almost there," he groans into my ear.

"Do it. Fucking wreck me. Make this hole yours, Janitor Boy!"

He reaches around me, shoulder over me, his biceps to my chest, and strokes me. Fast. Hard, he pulls my cock's foreskin up and down in his fist, which is slick with my pre-cum. I'm so close to bursting. It is too much. I can't hold it back any longer.

I come with a cry, biting into his shoulder to muffle it. He follows seconds later, hips thrusting into me, slurring my name like a prayer.

We collapse in a pile of limbs, sweat, and misplaced caution signs.

Silence. Breathing. The buzz of the overhead light.

Then — **CLUNK**.

A bottle of bleach rolls off a shelf and thuds to the ground by our feet.

"Sorry," I say, chuckling. "That might've been me. Gripped on too tight."□

Oscar laughs, deep and full. "We're gonna have to clean this whole place again."

"Good," I say. "I enjoy cleaning as long as you're here with me."

"You like me more," he teases.

I kiss him. "Always."

Outside the closet, the night carries on.

Inside, it is warm. Sacred. Ours.

There's a rumour around the office that my new employee, the new janitor Eddy, is a reincarnated soul.

There's another rumour that he hums to bins, and they hum back. That when he's happy, the trash bags float into the cart. He makes even the mop buckets blush. But I knew it was because he still possessed some of his Grouch abilities. He can still communicate with the Rot.

But no one can prove it.

Except me, who watches Eddy go about his cleaning. We often sneak off on trips to the janitor's closet when no one is looking.

All the employees know is that lately, the place shines more. Smells better. Feels lighter. And the Head of Cleaning Operations is finally smiling like he means it.

The finance department is always empty at night, except for two employees who seem to work overtime. I know them and just let them carry on, not disturbing them.

As I lock up the maintenance closet, I pass the break-room and overhear a peculiar conversation.

"...I'm just saying, Chase, you *can't* expense blood bags under 'client hospitality.'"

A sheepish laugh follows. "But Miles, they're O-negative, very premium!"

I smirk.

The new accountant is fussy. The vampire intern is a complete himbo. Classic Geek and Jock trope. And judging by the way their voices tangle in the fluorescent-lit air, something *messy* and *undeniably delicious* is brewing.

I nudge Eddy with my elbow.

"Wanna place bets on who catches feelings first?"

Eddy grins, eyes glinting like a full moon on bin juice. "Opposites attract, who will cave first."

We walk off laughing and never wondered if we were good enough for each other.

Sometimes you don't need a second chance.

You just need someone who sees you.

Really sees you.

And sometimes, miraculously, that someone crawls out of a bin.

The end.

The Haunt continues in...
Accounting on Him
A Vampire Himbo x Geeky Human
Accountant Opposites Attract Paranormal MM Romance

Bin There, Dumped That?

I had tried to keep a lid on it. I really did...

But there's one more scene that refused to be tossed...

A trashed story, if you will...

It didn't quite fit in the main story—too messy, too much... Grumble.

But I couldn't refuse it...Couldn't recycle it.

So, I'm taking out the trash one last time...

Get ready to dive into the Rot...

and re-bin-carnation chaos...

The Rot King's Rare Kindness

As dictated by His Supreme Grubbiness, King Grumble of the Rot

Y ou ever been woken up by the sound of a cursed jockstrap arguing with a discarded love letter? No? Must be nice.

I am curled up on my throne (read: a cracked bidet enshrined in banana peels), enjoying a well-earned nap when the walls of my kingdom start vibrating with spiritual whining.

Again.

"Grumble! Grumble!"

I don't bother looking up. I figure it's one of my servants. "Yes, yes, bring me offerings of rot and regret—" I look up. "Oh. It's you."

There stands *him*.

Eddy "Trash" Something.

Grouch-turned-soft.

Bin-boy Supreme.

"Grumble," he says, and—would you believe the audacity—he bows.

Like I am some kind of authority and not just the unfortunate immortal consequence of twenty-three failed reincarnations and a Subway footlong left under the sun too long.

"I need a favour," Eddy starts.

I cackle. I *howl*. I summon a choir of possessed pizza boxes just to sing "NO" in harmony. But the bastard waits till my dramatic performance is over to continue.

He waits with those gooey amber eyes and that *romance-novel-sacrificial-spirit* energy that makes me itch.

"A favour?" I spit, then I realise what is going on. He had changed. "You want a free reincarnation, don't you? You think this is some discount bin-reboot program?"

He doesn't flinch.

"Friend, please. I want to go back. I want to try again. As me. *Fully* me. Human. No more slime. No more rot. Just... a second chance."

Now, here's the thing. I *like* Eddy. Not enough to kiss his feet or anything—he's still tragically over-sentimental—but he's one of the few Bin-Spirits who didn't lose themselves in the muck or didn't try to crown themself *Lord of the Landfill* or build a temple out of old mattresses.

He fell in love. Broke a curse. Grew a soul.

Ugh. Gross.

But also... impressive.

So, I stand, all regal and sticky. Spread my arms wide like a raccoon pope and boom, "I, Grumble the Eternal, King of the Rot, declare this most uncommon of occasions—"

"—a Rare Kindness?" He asks.

My eyes shoot him a dirty look. Well, they always are dirty, but this is one of disdain. "Don't ruin my moment."

I summon the council; a sock puppet made of earwax, a dead pigeon whose owner used to do taxes, and the ghost of a half-eaten burrito.

They vote. Unanimously.

"He's annoying but kind of i-*coo*-nic," the pigeon says.

"Fine," I declare. "By the sovereign stench of my crown, I grant thee *The Rot's Rare Kindness*—one (1) human rebirth, at the age you died, to the year we are today. Limited warranty, no returns. If you die again, that's it."

Eddy blinks. "So... I'll live again?"

"You'll start fresh. Clean slate. New name, new paperwork, new social security number—"

"FUCK YEAH! I'm so happy, I could kiss-." Eddy runs up to me, and I hold my arms up in defence trying to bash him off.

"Whatever. Just don't come crying to me if it all goes to shit!"

Eddy grins.

He steps back and his body begins to glow. And in that final moment, before the rebirth bin shimmers open, he turns and says:

"Thank you, Grumble."

To which I reply, "Never speak of this again or I will flush your soul down a dimension where feelings are illegal."

Then he is gone.

Back to the mortal realm.

Back to the boy with the mop and the heartbreak.

Somewhere, in a world where the bins still clatter in moonlight, a new hire with amber eyes is clocking in for his first shift... and I, the royal rotted one, await the day my throne is challenged. The spirit realm of the Rot will now be unbalanced, unsettled, knowing that I had allowed one lucky soul to return. I hear the rumblings of a war brewing in the sewers.

But instead, I return to my throne. Bidet still cracked.

Empire still reeking.

But maybe, just *maybe*, the Rot isn't all bad.

First Look at Accounting On Him

Chase Von' Chasin' Johnson

Bro, pumping iron as a vampire is difficult. Not impossible, but you've gotta adjust. Like, first off, I can't go to the gym during the daylight hours anymore, unless I want to crisp up like a rotisserie chicken. Second? Apparently, a deep underground conspiracy aims to eliminate vampire bodybuilders, and they lace most protein powders with garlic powder.

What the fuck, right?

Humans are so petty. I've been a Fanger for six months, and I have absolutely seen the other side of how things are for us Vamps. Living was not only a chore, and most places were closed at night unless vampires ran them, but we also needed to find blood to quench our thirst.

Companies have tried to market synthetic blood, but not a single vamp would drink it. Unless they were Fegan—a Fanger Vegan. It became more of a derogatory term, and sorry to the Fegans, but I need to drink blood supplied from the source. Direct from the neck is most desirable, but trying to find a human who will offer their blood is like trying to find a job as a vampire.

Vampires going public meant that other supernaturals and not-supernaturals expected us to continue living with humans. *Witches, Bin-Spirits, Shifters* and even *Rock Band Demon Hunters* could go about their lives as per normal as if the entire supernatural world didn't just crack open.

I was in the middle of a DIY deadlift session in my apartment, using cinder blocks and a witch's broom I snagged from downstairs, squeezing my solid marble ass tight each bend, when the email I had been waiting for came in. My phone pinged on my blood-stained couch. Don't stress; the blood was from weeks ago during a *BF party*.

They called it bare fang as if we had tooth condoms for protection and chose not to wear them for the thrill, but it meant that we were siphoning blood directly from someone's neck. Of course, the people involved always give consent. I hated the taste of blood without consent.

Becoming a Fanger didn't improve my eyesight, sadly. It made me incredibly horny, almost frenzied, after a workout sesh, but the only other thing difficult to do as a vampire besides pumping iron is getting an erection naturally without the blood of our prospective sexual partner given willingly. I sighed, dropped my weights, which bounced with a loud clang, and I wiped my hands on the shirt I hung over a chair, then squinted at my screen.

> *Dear Mr Chase Johnson,*
> *Welcome to **VAMP-LINK** Supernatural Employment Services.*
> *Your placement has been assessed, and you have been successful in securing a role within Graves & Pennington Accounting as: Assistant Accountant*
> *Report to Mr Miles Penrose, Senior Accountant.*
> ***Time:** 8:30 PM sharp. DO NOT BE LATE. BRING ID, FANG REGISTRY CERTIFICATE AND YOUR THIRST FOR SUCCESS.*
> *(Note: thirst is metaphorical. Do not bite your manager.)*

I quickly got changed, no need to shower as vampires didn't have active sweat glands or body odour, and headed there.

I had a few hours until 8:30, so walked my way there. And the sun was down. It wasn't often I could enjoy walking inconspicuously.

Night time was our time as vamps. I never felt safer.

This would be my first job since, well...being bitten at the Nocturnal Gym. When I signed up, I didn't read the fine print. I apparently waived my right of consent. Being a human working out in a Fanger gym, I was fresh for the feasting.

But it wasn't my fault I joined a Fanger Gym; I have always been a night owl, and this was the best of both worlds. I barely made it through my first gym sesh, spotting a bulky muscle god of a man when I felt something on my neck. The asshole bit me. Took my blood and put his venom in me, against my wishes. I am just thankful I could keep my agency. Most newborn vamps must bend themselves to the will of their changers, the vampires who infect their victims with vampirism, but the form I signed allowed me to keep my own wits.

Since then, I have had an insatiable lust for blood and bulking up. I've always been gay. Becoming a Vamp has only made me appreciate the male form even more.

I was attempting to keep my cool as I finished checking over the email. My heart, well it would if it still beat without feasting on blood, fell through my ass as I saw the words I didn't originally see in the email. There in the email the words ' *BUSINESS CASUAL*' revealed themselves. As if they were taped off like a crime scene, with flashing lights and two police officers on either side directing my eyes to 'move along'.

I was dressed in grey sweatpants, which revealed everything, a black tank that read "Fanger Pride", a backwards cap and, to top it all off, 'New Balances'.

Yes. This vampire wears dad sneakers. I liked comfort. I liked good arch support. And they were squeaking against the tiled floor, practically announcing my anxiety to the receptionist. She looked up, and she gave me a disgruntled look, like I had just interrupted her performing a séance.

"Ah!" She smirked. She had long brown hair and a look that made me feel she could see ghosts hanging around me. "You're the new Vamp-link hire. Mr Johnson"

"That's me."

She was looking me up and down. "Interesting attire. Guess business casual means something different for vampires."

"I didn't see it in the email until I walked in."

"Try to wear a business shirt and chinos next time, here." She handed me a card in a plastic sleeve. "This is your pass into the Accounting office; don't mind the janitor; he will just tend to the floors and clean out the bins at his own leisure."

I raised an eyebrow. "Okay then."

"Head on through the lifts and go to level four. Mr Penrose awaits you."

I did as she instructed, my new balances squeaking the entire time I headed to the lift foyer. This was one of those modern office buildings, and I didn't need to press a single button for the elevator to work.

I was thoroughly impressed and even let out an amused hum as the elevator arrived on the ground floor. I entered the mirrored little box. I wouldn't have known I was awake, because vampires don't have reflections in mirrors. That was common knowledge, right? It was news to me at first, and I freaked-the-fuck-out.

Olden day vampires had never seen what they became, but modern vamps are spoiled. In our gyms and with special Vampiric socials and apps, we can see ourselves. From enchanted mirrors to modern witch-tech apps, the life of a modern vampire is pretty comfortable.

Between Vampstagram, FangFace and the one app that has sat on my phone way too long, Fang2Bang—a gay vampire dating app. It is sordid—I feel little different from I did as a human. The users on the dating apps are filthy; all want to be bitten and used as blood slaves. They needed an exorcist.

I looked back where I assumed my reflection would normally be, and I pulled faces. I stuck out my tongue and even tempted to pull down my pants just enough to show my ass in the jockstrap I had on. But I resisted as I noticed the camera.

I let the elevator take me to level four, and it wasn't long until the elevator made a ding and the doors opened.

The level was entirely different from the ground floor foyer. *Graves & Pennington* really lived up to its grave part of its name.

Dreary. Grey. All The same.

My vampiric sight enhanced colours, but even that was no help. Rows upon rows of desks, like it was a graveyard, and each desktop screen was a tombstone. The nameplates on each partition were the only separators for each desk; otherwise, they were identical to a fault. I stepped out, bracing for cubicle hell, and walked straight into *him*.

And I mean *straight* into him. Shoulders, chest, hot coffee splashed over both of us. A very startled yelp, not mine as I don't feel pain from hot liquids. As I apologised, I received a death glare that could've fried the flesh off my body met my own.

If I had breath left in my body, he would've knocked the wind right out of me.

Tall. Stern. Unsmiling. Hair the colour of bitter espresso—which only made me miss my morning lattes even more. His eyes were darker. Cheekbones that could end wars. Forearms that I would lick and trace his veins. He was the kind of guy you only ever saw yelling at interns in a legal drama or starring in some cheap, piece of crap, gay indie film about an accountant falling for a vampire colleague; they were my secret pleasure.

I was getting carried away and practically walking down the aisle with this man, and I haven't even introduced myself.

I froze.

My fangs nearly extended as my body detected an attack. My brain short circuiting at how much this man made my bloodless heart pump.

"I assume you are the new hire?" He asked as he brushed off his shirt, flicked his hand and then wiped it on the back of his pants.

His eyes took me in and scanned the coffee damage between us.

"I—uh—yes," I stammered. I wanted to be suave and attempted to lean, but I almost stumbled and went flying into the cubicle wall near me. "Chase Johnson. *VampLink* sent me."

He blinked once. Then again. Slow. Calculated. Judging. Counting his moments.

"Why are you wearing sweatpants? Did you not read Business Casual?"

"I didn't read the email closely enough..."

"Your shirt says Fanger Pride."

"Pride is never casual." I replied solemnly.

He stared at me in pure, undiluted silence.

And then, with a weary sigh of a man who'd already had three coffees, none of which appeared to be strong enough, he said, "I'm Miles Penrose. You will report to me. Follow me and try not to bump into anything else." He pointed between the coffee stains and everything around him.

I immediately let my fingers glide across the fabric of the divider walls as I followed him.

He glared backwards. "I said nothing, Mr Johnson."

"Oh, sorry." I sheepishly replied and scratched the back of my head. Some human habits die hard.

He turned sharply at a fork in the dividers, and I followed behind like a lost puppy being lured with a meal.

We passed the rows of desks, my sneakers squeaking with each turn like a rubber chicken at a funeral. Miles didn't say a word. Just walked.

Stiff. Seething. Like he regretted every life choice that brought him here tonight.

"Do I get a welcome pack?" I asked brightly trying to defuse the tension. "Some bat-shaped paperclips? A spreadsheet I can sink my fangs into?"

He stopped, walked. Turned. Faced me with the same stern look.

"You're here to observe and file. And only assist with budgets when I feel you are ready. Breathe too loud and you'll be assigned to Crypt Audit. Is that clear?"

I saluted. "Loud and clear. Vampires don't breathe, boss man."

"Don't call me that."

'Roger, Chief Number guy!"

His eye twitched. "Come, our desks are over here." He turned back around, and I paused as he walked ahead.

I might be undead, but this man had me feeling things that were absolutely not safe for the workplace. Good thing I had to be invited in, or I would have taken this man on a desk in a heartbeat. Good thing I don't have a heartbeat. Well, not without some fresh blood, but I think Miles only had budgets on the mind.

Stay on the lookout for more soon!

Acknowledgements

Or as I call it, a look back at what a fucking year I had!

2025 has been a year unlike any other. Back when I was writing *Dad Magic* in 2023-2024, I had no idea what was in store for me on the day of release. 28 November 2024, my boss of 6 years passed away. **Karen Collins** was a beautiful human being. So kind and warm. She would always bake for us in her team. She would tell me stories about her children. The most detailed stories that rivaled even a purple prose pro. Not a day has gone by since her passing that I haven't missed her. She was my shoot the shit person. We would just talk anything. Without judgement. She was a mother. A fighter until the end.

I remember the final dream I had of Karen. She was dressed in a beautiful purple silk ball gown and looked fucking fantastic. She was glowing. She invited me into her office and then looked at me with the most heartbreaking yet comforting smile I could imagine. She said to me a few simple words. *"Well that's it. I am off."* she paused and turned to me then said *"I'm ok."* She then turned and phased through her office wall and disappeared.

From that moment I haven't dreamt of her. I believe dreams tell us things our human brains cannot fathom. I am not a religious person anymore, but to me this signalled her passing over to the other side. To the great Ballroom.

She was ok. She was no longer in pain.

Thank you Karen for all your lessons you gave me over those six years. Thank you for saving me from the worst job I had ever been in. And thank you for always being a shoulder to cry on, an ear to listen, a friend to be there for us all. I miss you, but you are forever in our hearts.

I chose the release of 28 November 2025 for *Can't Refuse Him* to signify my change into Romance, and to remind myself this book would not exist if I had no experienced this last year. Grief has a funny way of bringing the best out of you.

I'd like to acknowledge my editor, **Jacob Sinne**, who stepped up and really took this book from trash to treasure. It was such a great experience to work with you on this project. You challenged me in ways I could not imagine and really brought me to my best with this book.

To **Moody Bitches, the best author group chat**, each and every one of you, you were there during the birth of this story and now here as well standing alongside me as I bring it into the world fully realised.

My alpha and beta readers, my early ARC readers, and my ARC readers in general. Thank you for reading, enjoying, crying and laughing with my boys Oscar and Eddy.

Chloe, you have been one of my greatest supporters in my indie journey. To think if you never signed up for *Dad Magic* where both of our lives would be! I am eternally grateful for your friendship and trust. Meeting you also was fantastic and felt like being at home. I cannot wait to see you again at BBE and many more book events!

Brendan, thank you for making this year bearable on Bookstagram! Your wisdom and graphic knowledge as well as all the laughs we have shared!

Richard, you make me laugh so fucking much everyday! Your dry british humour really got me through 2025!

To **Desmond,** the first reader of all my books. You are truly one of the greatest people ever! Don't let it go to your head though! Love you!

Lastly, **Aleks.** My Love. This story is a dedication to the strength you have given me to fight through this past year. From the simple being at my side in silent strength, holding me when I am crying at the smallest emotional scenes in movies, to building me back up after the many grief stricken breakdowns. You are what anchors me when I start floating. You are my wind to my fire to let it burn bright.

To **Venus,** you get me full time again for a while! All the pats and love cuddles!

And lastly to *Oscar and Eddy,* for reminding us all that we are not trash!

About the author

Benjamin Twigg is a fantasy and romance writer from Australia. As a queer author, Ben strives to write stories that have authentic representation, queer joy and a sense of wonder. □

As a child, Ben dreamed of being a fantasy author and dived into those books, devouring the stories and world they created. As an adult, his love for fantasy world-building continued with role-playing video games, and he has racked up hundreds of hours of gameplay, immersing himself in character stories with amazing arcs.□

Benjamin now also writes paranormal MM romance featuring monsters, ghostly boyfriends, ghoulish gays and sad-bois desperate for connection under the pen name B. J. Twigg□

You can find Ben making whimsical memes and reels on Instagram or spending time with his beloved dog, and his partner. □

Follow the author on social media by scanning the below QR Code.